Early Praise for
Cryptids, Kaiju & Corn

"Dangers gather like evocative whispers along natural and unnatural bloodlines of the Midwest in *Cryptids, Kaiju & Corn*. An extraordinary anthology, the visceral heartbeats of grit, horror, and rural life come together to linger provocatively on the reader's mind."

—Sirrah Medeiros,
author of the novels *The Malediction Plague* and *Secrets of Mother*,
and editor of *Don't Ask, Ghosts Tell: An LGBTQ+ Horror Anthology*
and *The Haunted Zone: A Horror Anthology
by Women Military Veterans*

"Poems to unsettle. Stories to unnerve. A collection that haunts, challenges, and frames anew a region that should perhaps be renamed 'the dark heartland of America.' Read these with the lights on and one eye on the window!"

—Travis Klempan,
author of the supernaturally tinged novels
Have Snakes, Need Birds and *Hills Hide Mountains*

"Looking for a spooky read? Settle in on a moonless night with *Cryptids, Kaiju & Corn*, but pay no mind to the blood-red eyes watching from the window or the ragged claw tracing down your neck. Filled with poems to pierce your soul and flash-fiction to send shivers down your spine, *Cryptids, Kaiju & Corn* is the perfect book for the cryptid-curious reader who doesn't mind losing a little sleep. You'll find no pumpkin-spice lattes here. It's monster season!"

—Brett Allen,
author of the Midwest cryptid novel *Sly Fox Hollow*,
as well as the GWOT service comedy *Kilroy Was Here*

Also from Middle West Press LLC

anthologies

Giant Robot Poems:
On Mecha-Human Science, Culture & War
Edited by Randy Brown

Our Best War Stories:
Prize-winning Poetry & Prose
from the Col. Darron L. Wright Memorial Awards, Vols. 1 & 2
Edited by Christopher Lyke

Why We Write:
Craft Essays on Writing War
Edited by Steve Leonard and Randy Brown

Things We Carry Still:
Poems & Micro-Stories about Military Gear
Edited by Lisa Stice and Randy Brown

Midwest Futures:
Poems & Micro-Stories from Tomorrow's Heartland
Edited by Randy Brown

poetry collections

The Explosion Takes Both Legs: Noir Poems from the War in Iraq
by J.B. Stevens

Paying for Gas with Quarters: A Parent's Odyssey in Poems
by Aly Allen

Cryptids, Kaiju & Corn

Poems and Micro-Stories
about
Modern Midwest Monsters

Edited by Randy Brown
Middle West Press LLC
Johnston, Iowa

Literary Anthology / Fantasy, Sci-Fi & Horror / U.S. Midwest

ISBN (print): 978-1-953665-34-8
ISBN (e-book): 978-1-953665-35-5
Library of Congress Control Number: 2025947081

Middle West Press LLC
P.O. Box 1153
Johnston, Iowa 50131-9420

Connect with us on-line:
linktr.ee/MiddleWestPress

"[...] A pale glow stole over the Thing;
gradually its cloudy folds took shape—
an arm appeared, then legs, then a body,
and last a great sad face looked out of the vapor.
Stripped of its filmy housings, naked, muscular and comely,
the majestic Cardiff Giant loomed above me!

All my misery vanished—for a child might know that no harm
could come with that benignant countenance. My cheerful spirits returned
at once, and in sympathy with them the gas flamed up brightly again.
Never a lonely outcast was so glad to welcome company
as I was to greet the friendly giant!"

—Mark Twain, "A Ghost Story" (1870)

CONTENTS

Squonks, Squawks, & Sirens

Neighbors, Stones, & Curses

Discussion & Writing Prompts

About the Editor

Foreword

At Middle West Press, we like to complicate people's perceptions of what it means to live, work, and play in the American Midwest—as well as what it means to put down roots, or to claim it as a place of origin.

That goes for dark and seedy stuff, too. Midwesterners—even our city folk—like to reap what we sow.

Giants still walk our flat and rolling lands, and swim in our deep lakes and rivers. Ask around any truck stop or diner, and you'll likely meet or hear-tell of frog people. Dog men. Wendigo spirits.

We have danced in the headlights with faeries and farmhands. We have tipped cows under the harvest moon. We have walked the streets, long after they've rolled up the sidewalks.

Even our endless, flyover-skies contain ancient and thunderous birds. Remember that, as you run to your next airport connections in Minneapolis-St. Paul, Chicago, or St. Louis. Keep those seatbelts tight!

This book collects more than 70 short poems and 300-word narratives of mythic beasts that illuminate, celebrate, or challenge stereotypes of Midwestern identity.

To motivate both writers and readers, starting on page 130, the anthology also includes a special section of 7 discussion-starters and prompts, for use in writing workshops, book clubs, and other gatherings.

We hope that you enjoy your time with the Middle West. Just remember: It's complicated. And sometimes, downright scary.

—Randy "Sherpa" Brown

Little Houses,
Dark Harvests

The Harvest Men
by John Tyler Leonard

Way out of town, a little further than the county line,
when it's so hot that even the birds don't sing,
we plant our dead in stone gardens and leave out
bottles of cold beer for the Harvest Men.

The Harvest Men take up a sort of dancing, hand-in-hand
as they sway in circles to their own breathless silence.
They wriggle and grin like dried up worms.
They hold out slender hands, invite you over,
and not just at midnight.

Some folks are lost to the Harvest Men's traditions;
out-of-towners caught unaware. But we know. We know
because we are part of the knowing. Windows kept shut,
all through August. Children with their forward gazes.
We know to hold our breath everywhere we go.

That's how the Harvest Men like it.
Their name on the wind, being whispered about.
They like to be seen out of the corner of a church boy's eye,
smelled in the afternoon air. Tasted.

Did you know they sweat?
Did you know how much they sicken our summers?
How sweet they are on the breeze?

That's just how they like it; when the grass stops growing
and it's so hot that the shadow of a tombstone looks inviting.
That's when they'll gesture and wave, but only to the ones
who don't know, the ones who will take the Harvest Men's hands,

peel off their own skin and hang it on a tree, the ones who will
do that strange sort of dance.

They don't know,
but we know.

John Tyler Leonard is a writer, educator, editor-in-chief of Rawhead, *and managing editor of 42 Miles Press and* The Glacier. *He holds a graduate degree in English from Indiana University. His poems have been published in* Chiron Review, December Magazine, North Dakota Review, Ethel Zine, Louisiana Literature, Jelly Bucket, Painted Bride Quarterly, Tipton Poetry Journal, Qu Literary Magazine, Hole in The Head Review, Nimrod International Journal, The Indianapolis Review, Two Hawks Quarterly, The Emerson Review, *and many others. Leonard was the 2016 inaugural recipient of the Wolfson Poetry Award, the 2018 recipient of the Josephine K. Piercy Memorial Award, and the 2019 recipient of the David E. Albright Memorial Award and Hatfield Merit Award. He lives in Elkhart, Indiana with his wife and son. Visit: www.instagram.com/jotyleon*

Hum/Chirp
by Maggie Dow

On the day he comes to town, he blots out the sun. They'll talk about it for decades.

His wings spread, thunderstorm-black, against the periwinkle Nebraska summer sky, casting a nearly opaque shadow over the speck on the map that is Bartleby. On the farms outside of town, chickens return to roost, cattle bed down in the fields, and children run home from their imagined enchanted forests. In Bartleby, some folks dive for cover in their basement storm shelters when the sky goes dark. Others peer through windows and step out through shop doors into the street, eyes turned heavenward, mouths helplessly agape.

No one has ever seen anything like him. They've heard stories, but the truth in stories is rarely fact. No one believed them. No one expected ... this.

He touches down on the far end of Marshall Street with a celluloid crunch. A gnashing whirl vibrates in the stale air, a thrumming disquiet that ripples through town. His skin is an armored carapace, his eyes oblong and shiny-black, his antenna thin and reaching. Someone unsheathes their cell phone, ready to post a Snapchat, a TikTok, something, desperate to preserve the evidence before their eyes. He is here. He is real and he is horrible.

If this was somewhere else, he would be called something different. Any farther east and people would whisper behind their hands that they had seen Mothman. Farther north, they might call him a thunderbird. There are a thousand names for whatever he is, no two the same, no one completely right. Here on the farm-dotted plains of Nebraska, where people still carry the genetic scars left by their ancestors' dust-rimmed lungs, memories stretch back to the 19th century. Bartleby still remembers knee-high grasshoppers, so here, there is only one name for him.

Locust.

Maggie Dow was born and raised in South Dakota, but has always been inspired by the stories and landscapes of the broader American West. An environmental educator, folk music fan, and lover of all things spooky, Dow's writing is influenced by her experiences in and love for America's wide-open spaces. Her fiction blends the mundane and macabre, exploring the intersections of place, identity, and the unknown. Her work has been published in Oakwood.

The Day of the Sunflowers
by Brittany Redd

A nice plot of land for another agricultural Megacorp
to bend to their will; a sunflower field
with no buildings on it
No sense in leaving an empty space.

Megacorp leaves its mark in the shape
of a sharp logo, a new gray square on the horizon
and the latest chemtech,
    t
     r

                i
                  c
                k
                    ling down into the soil.

They deigned to install the cameras after the night guards said they saw
shadows lurking in the distance. Didn't look human. Probably a coyote.
Didn't look like a coyote.

Root-like limbs break
through glass, creeping
into the pores of
the cheap foundation.

More dust for the soil.

From the seeds of their fallen brethren,
the sunflowers
              e
            s
         o
       r
What couldn't kill them

made them stronger, ready to take back their lot.

Brittany Redd (she/they) grew up in Kansas, but now teaches and writes in Thailand. Their work appears or is forthcoming in Funicular Magazine, Corvid Queen, ephemeras, Litmora, *and elsewhere.*

Locust of Control
by Gabrielle Rabon

June approaches, and the not-girl feels it in their chest: the ceaseless drum, the rhythmic drone, the snap of newly formed muscles. Summer cicadas flex their transforming bodies, the sound of their sexuality permeating the humid air.

Their song fills the not-girl with anticipation, at once unknowably ancient and entirely present. And as they hear the click and tick and *tszzt-tszzt*, they begin to crawl through the grass.

They reach out their forelegs, pulling themselves up and up and up. They sit high in the branches and press their face against the trunk, the rough bark scratching at their cheek. The not-girl feels the selfsame hum, the cicada's buzz and pop and click-click-click, calling back out to them from deep within their own soft form.

Around them, thousands of cicadas wriggle and thrash against the trees, freeing themselves of the nymphish bodies that no longer suit them. The not-girl arches their back and flexes their shoulders—soon they too will shed their skin and their own wings will unfurl, ready for flight.

As the not-girl watches, the cicadas turn their red eyes on them. The not-girl feels no fear as the insects silently observe; they recognize the not-girl as one of their own. As they wait, the hum grows louder. It drowns out the not-girl's human thoughts until all they know is sound and earth and tree and sky and ...

Finally they are content.

Like the other cicadas, the not-girl is preparing to emerge from their larval state. Soon that which is inside them will stretch and pull and rip, and they will spill out of their body, out of their womanhood, into themself. Like a cloud of locusts, their queerness will blanket the earth: a blessed pestilence, filling the air with its limitless, joyful song.

Gabrielle Rabon (she/they/he) is a queer writer and media professional based in Chicago. Growing up adjacent to a nature preserve in Michigan, they spent much of their childhood outside climbing trees, watching bugs and making houses for the fairies. Through their writing, Rabon seeks to better understand the human condition, with a specific focus on gender, sexuality, and bodily autonomy.

The Cornfather
by Tyler Stallings

Dale's crop is dying. Leaves curl, stalks crack, roots claw at dust. He's got one shot left. A plastic sack, no label, stolen from the lab where his cousin cleans floors. A "miracle hybrid," they said. Stronger than drought. Stronger than anything to survive living in the town of Silos End.

He plants at midnight. Bare hands, pressing each seed deep. No rain, no hope, just this. A silent prayer: Grow. Please.

By dawn, the field is alive. Stalks thick as fence posts, leaves sharp as razors. The air smells wrong—wet metal, overripe fruit. The wind moves jagged, stops and starts, like something breathing through clenched teeth.

By noon, the whispering starts.

Not wind.

"Son."

Dale stills.

The husks shift, splitting open. A voice spills out, slow, stretched. A voice that left twenty years ago and never came back.

"Dad?"

A stalk bows. Something inside bulges, pressing against green skin. Dale reaches. Peels back the husk.

Teeth. Yellowed, wet. A mouth. The corn breathes.

The whole field exhales. More husks split, more mouths open. Wet, sucking gasps. Voices rising, weaving. Mom. Grandpa. Coach Tim from high school. The old dog he buried behind the barn.

The land was starving. Dale fed it too much.

He stumbles back. The stalks bend, reaching. Roots stretch beneath his boots, groping.

The screen door creaks. Mary steps onto the porch, barefoot, breath hitching.

The whispering shifts. A baby's gurgle. Soft. Sweet. Three summers gone. Small bones under the cottonwood.

Mary sways. Steps forward. One hand to her mouth. The other reaching, reaching—
Dale grabs her wrist. Holds tight.
The field groans. The husks shudder.
Something under the soil wakes, hungry.

Tyler Stallings, a Southern California-based writer, is the author of Aridtopia: Essays on Art & Culture from Deserts in the Southwest United States. *He is also a contributor or editor of anthologies, including:* Whiteness: A Wayward Construction; Mundos Alternos: Art and Science Fiction in the Americas; *and* Uncontrollable Bodies: Testimonies of Identify and Culture. *His stories and essays have appeared in* Southwest Contemporary, Los Angeles Review, *PBS Socal's* "Artbound," Citric Acid, *and* Tendon. *Visit: www.tylerstallings.com*

The Motherhouse
by Molly Gustafson

The stone path winding toward the Motherhouse
is paved in the rouge tint of gutted fish.
Those steps intermingle the deep-growing moss
with the abattoir's most obedient and dutiful flesh.

Does the Mother store my bones in jam jars?
Does she taste my ribbon-sinew like the honeysuckle
that grows in her garden? This is a house you dare
yourself to leave because piety here will wrinkle

your individuality and pierce a tooth
through your resolve. Mother is coconut-
cream sweet, but pages made of wolf
skin line her gospel. She will tie a knot

in your squirming belly and call you her diamond.
Mother is immutable: carnivorous and holy fiend.

*Molly Gustafson is a senior undergraduate student at Lewis University,
Romeoville, Illinois. She studies writing and theater. In her spare time,
Gustafson enjoys singing, dancing, and being in nature.*

Cryptid Convention
by Rhonda Havig

Walking into a small patch of woods near Wisner Road, I spot a shack in shambles. Approaching it, I check the flyer I'd found while walking under the crybaby bridge and verify this is the location of the CryptiCon.

For the past few days, I've imagined meeting the legends I've only read about on the internet when sneaking into the Kirtland Public Library at night. I wonder if Grassman, the Frogmen, and the Wolfman of Defiance will be equally excited to meet a Melonhead like me.

I pull the latch string on the shack's door, which clicks and creaks ajar. Pushing it fully open, I step inside. Music pulses below me. Light filters through the floorboards. Elation fills my heart.

Finding the stairs, I descend into a delightful conclave of cryptids. I wish my fellow Melonheads had joined me to enjoy this amazing sight!

The last step squeaks, drawing everyone's attention toward me.

I gaze across the room at the collection of creatures. The Frogmen are taller and thinner than I expected. And Grassman is much shorter. The Wolfman's fur looks kinda fake. Are those Pukwudgies? I didn't think they were real.

Stepping forward through the crowd are a couple of Melonheads. Did my friends acquiesce and attend after all?

As they move closer, I realize I don't recognize them. And their heads look like … is that rubber?

Eyes wide, they reach out to touch me, but I back up into the wall.

That's when it hits me: these aren't cryptids.

Rhonda Havig is an Ohio-based writer. She grew up being told Bigfoot lived on her family's property in southwest Missouri. She has contributed to the "Creepy" podcast, the University of Dayton Magazine, *and* Literary Mama, *where she has also served as managing editor.*

The Road That Calls My Name:
The Beast of Bray Road Speaks
by Nicole Antillon

I was not always this.
I had a name, A voice, A place at the fire.
Now, I have a mouth full of knives.

The change was not a choice.
It was hunger.
It was the snap of a spine under a harvest moon,
the sound of something ancient pressing its fingers into my ribs,
peeling me open, whispering run, run, run.

I did RUN, CHASE, HUNT
and I never stopped.

They call me monster.
I call them prey.

They come searching,
clutching their shotguns, their silver bullets, their prayers,
as if the old stories will save them.

As if anything will.

I crouch in the ditches, belly to the mud,
watching headlights carve through the dark.
They roll up their windows when the radio crackles,
lock their doors at the first whisper of wind.

As if glass can stop me.

As if I need an invitation.

They will not see me,
not until they do.
Not until the breath stills in their throat,
not until the scream curdles against the pines,
not until their bones are cooling in the dirt—

And by then,
I will already be inside,
ripping at their pleading cries.

I do not knock.
I do not ask.
I do not leave witnesses.

I was not always this.
Now, this is all I am.
Not a shred of holy light left.

but the road,
the road still calls my name.

Nicole Antillon is single, working mother from Phoenix, Arizona whose work delves into themes of mythology, transformation, healing, and identity. Visit: www.winglessdreamer.com

postcard to the nine voles i met outside the Speedway on Four Mile
by Liam Strong

i heard someone the other day call you field mice, which feels too rural & midwestern, let alone taxonomically incorrect. my blood is cold all the time, for instance, especially when my lips are at their most quiet, especially when i'm not who people say i am. it's so human, isn't it. you don't have names for you, so you just are, which feels like something Descartes or Voltaire would be proud of, but it's rare to find someone with mirth toward you. i sometimes find myself wanting to be a vole. you'd say though that i could never be one. you are scared, as you should be. i'm the devil, i'm uncooked meat, i'm more cryptid than mammalia. philosophers have demanded the uniqueness of humanity, mainly for the ability of complex thought. it's not unique, it's not complex, because i'm angry & i'm thankful & i'm thankful i can be angry. i eat flesh like & unlike myself, which is why i stop at places like gas stations. i'm there to never be a regular, to always be a traveler when i'm, in fact, always just right here, waiting for headlights to tell me where my humanity really lies.

Liam Strong (they/them) is a queer neurodivergent cripple punk writer who has earned an undergraduate degree in writing from University of Wisconsin-Superior. They are the author of the chapbook Everyone's Left the Hometown Show *(Bottlecap Press). You can find their poetry and essays in Vagabond City and new words {press}, among several others. They are almost likely gardening and listening to Bitter Truth somewhere in Northern Michigan. Visit: linktr.ee/liamstrong666*

The Family Farm
by Seán Betzer

Emma threw open the farmhouse's back door. Times like these called for a shotgun. Why didn't she have a shotgun? Not that she'd use one.

Midnight had come and gone. Floodlights illuminated the area directly around the house and the overcast sky blocked the moonlight that might otherwise light the rest of the cornfield.

Emma clenched her fists. She would be scared, but she knew who had taken her son. He didn't scare her.

"Ben took William," she told the corn. "Please. Help me find them."

No wind blew and, yet, the scarecrow at the edge of the floodlights swiveled on its mounting. One sleeve fluttered. Corn stalks bowed away from each other, creating a path. Emma turned on her phone's flashlight, then raced into the field.

The path led her left and right as her quarry twisted through the corn. One, two minutes passed before she found them at the second scarecrow. Billy sat on the ground at its feet while his father thrashed in the thing's arms.

Emma's heart pounded. She checked her 6-year-old son was all right, then turned to her husband. In the light of her phone's flashlight, she could see his pale skin and wide, terror-filled eyes.

"Let me go!" he shouted, fighting the scarecrow's hold. "*Grr!* How, how is it doing this? It can't be this strong. It's just straw!"

"Calm down, Ben."

"I can't stand it! Noises all night. Furniture moving on its own. The kitchen's always—"

"I told you, Ben. The farm is haunted. But it protects us."

"You call this protection?"

"I call it a timeout. Now, will you calm down and come back to bed, or do I need to ask my ancestor's ghost to hold you here all night?"

Seán Betzer lives in Portland, Oregon, where he works from home under the supervision of a ginger tabby tomcat and a laid-back black cat assistant. At least once a week, the tom reminds him that cats were once worshipped as gods. Visit: scribbalqwill.bsky.social

Daytime Hauntings
by John Tyler Leonard

Looney Tunes is playing on the parlor TV.
What concerns me is the power is out.
These days have their own, unique sense of
humor.

Today is colorless, but also a flower.
It's a windmill dragon and leftover chop suey
that has tragically become self-aware and
a pale, ugly fish that sucks the algae off
a paler, somehow even uglier fish.

The day fills your house with the least amount
of light that it can, from a legal perspective.

Notice how some houses will ask you to wait before
moving to another room, like you're a child again,
waiting for the adults to sweep up broken glass or
wipe blood from a split lip or swat the clenched teeth
humidity out of the air.

The day is a white bedsheet drifting down the stairs,
floating to the kitchen, and turning on the faucet,
all while you sit in your reading chair, drooling
in disbelief, or a whimsical kind of horror
that's difficult to describe.

The day has you under a blanket, frozen in fear,
just waiting for the sun to go down, so the power
will come back on and relieve you from a haunting
that keeps odd hours.

John Tyler Leonard is a writer, educator, editor-in-chief of Rawhead, *and managing editor of 42 Miles Press and* The Glacier. *He holds a graduate degree in English from Indiana University. His poems have been published in* Chiron Review, December Magazine, North Dakota Review, Ethel Zine, Louisiana Literature, Jelly Bucket, Painted Bride Quarterly, Tipton Poetry Journal, Qu Literary Magazine, Hole in The Head Review, Nimrod International Journal, The Indianapolis Review, Two Hawks Quarterly, The Emerson Review, *and many others. Leonard was the 2016 inaugural recipient of the Wolfson Poetry Award, the 2018 recipient of the Josephine K. Piercy Memorial Award, and the 2019 recipient of the David E. Albright Memorial Award and Hatfield Merit Award. He lives in Elkhart, Indiana with his wife and son. Visit: www.instagram.com/jotyleon*

The Inner Life of Objects
by David Clink

*"We often feel elation reading Neruda because he follows some arc of
association which corresponds to the inner life of objects."*
—Robert Bly (*Leaping Poetry*, 1972)

The path I walked to your door held
my hesitation, vanishings of feet
that uneasily rose from their footfalls.
The path lifted emotion from latent prints
which held Precambrian memories,
rocky beginnings, a molten past
that tried too hard to be profound,
the sun's sarcasm,
the moon's tranquility.
The path retained the footprints of a Nebraska
Bigfoot that rose out of its mistakes.
And it led to a room with:
1] five garbage bags, all tagged and ready
to be put out in the morning
to avoid overnight raccoons;
2] a washing machine and a dryer—
witnesses to the best and worst of us; and
3] a Schwinn bicycle gathering dust.
Each object is imbued with some element of us—
a plaster cast of a Bigfoot imprint
found on a riverbed reminded us
that we had tread where so many others had,
on a planet in a decaying orbit
around a dying star, as we spoke

the language of unsaid things.

David Clink's poem "A sea monster tells his story" won the 2013 Aurora Award for Best Poem/Song. Clink's latest collection is The Black Ship *(Aeolus House). Visit: davidlivingstoneclink.com*

Jack O' Lantern
by Lauren Breen

Carve a face, get every detail right,
down to the half-smile
and crescent irises (paint them blue).
Dig out the guts, stringy and wet,
perfect for hair and grease.
Carve until the bottom is flat.
Place a candle there and watch
the image burst into light.
But the flame burns out, the flesh
grows cold, and rot begins. It starts
at the edges of the eyes and lips,
collapses into itself.
Watch as I toss it away.

Lauren Breen received an undergraduate degree in creative writing from Susquehanna University, Selinsgrove, Pennsylvania. There, she read for the writing program's literary magazine, Rivercraft, *as well as the student run literary magazine,* Sanctuary. *She moved to Pittsburgh in 2012, and received her MFA in poetry at Chatham University in 2015. She became involved in Madwomen in the Attic writing workshop shortly after graduating. Her work has or will appear in* Voices from the Attic, Dionne's Story, *and* Plants and Poetry Journal.

The Soyote
by Patrick M. Hare

At first we didn't believe the kids' tales of weird camouflage coyotes lurking in the junk piled around the abandoned Thai restaurant. Why would we? Kids make up all kinds of outlandish stuff, and while we knew coyotes were around, blurring past our headlights when we got home from the bar and howling back at emergency sirens, it's not like they typically posed to be gawked at by a gaggle of middle-schoolers. Ephemerality defines them. Add in the amount of refuse crowding the restaurant, even before it became a clandestine dump for industrial waste, and it would be odd if kids didn't conjure weird shapes in the shadows. But then we too started to have encounters with the disguised canids: a fence line with a snout and too many uprights; the shadow of a bushy dog on the ground next to a wall with no caster; a lazy flick of pink tongue from the center of the gas station wall. Either Eugene Chess's soybean field next to the Thai restaurant seemed to be a popular hangout or the soybeans had started growing sporadic fluffy stalks at twilight. "Chameleyote" was explored as a name, but "soyote" was easier to say while also capturing their propensity to absorb the flavor of their surroundings. The soyotes soon became familiar, occasionally given resident status. Then Cayleigh Jenkins' toddler went missing, and panic flashed through the town (her disreputable ex's simultaneous disappearance was ignored). The Chess field became a nighttime shooting gallery. A trap offered up a spindly foam-textured leg. Somehow no one witnessed the restaurant burn down, despite a suspicious concentration of smoky laundromat loads. After that, the town exhaled and sightings decreased, but coyotes have adapted to us too well to truly leave. Some nights my shed has a tail, and I'm glad.

Patrick M. Hare has had words appear in such publications as Gordon Square Review, iō Literary Journal, Bookends Review, Vestal Review, *and the scientific journal* Photochemistry and Photobiology. *They are mostly good words and only a few are made up. He lives near Cincinnati, Ohio. Visit: pmhare.wordpress.com*

We Don't Go Outside Anymore, Because of the Not-Deer
by Juleigh Howard-Hobson

They looked so calm, we never thought they were
fur covered monsters instead of deer. Who
knew such things could exist, and would wander
around Missouri? We intended to
shoo them out, but they surrounded us while
smiles formed on their faces and pointed fangs
sprang from their lips. There was a horrible
vile smell, like forgotten flesh when it hangs
rank and rotting, from a butcher's hook. They
stayed there, growling they would eat us, and we
believed them. Suddenly, they leaped away,
spraying loose garden soil and laughing. Bees
freely hummed in the cherry blooms, the sun
hung from the sky, yet normal life was done.

Juleigh Howard-Hobson's speculative poetry has appeared in The Deadlands, 34 Orchard, Midnight Echo, Star*Line, Siren's Call, The Audient Void, Silver Blade, Vastarien: Women's Horror *(Grimscribe Press),* Under Her Skin *(Black Spot), and many other places. Her latest poetry collection is* Curses, Black Spells & Hexes *(Alien Buddha). She is an active member of the Horror Writers Association (HWA), and the Science Fiction and Fantasy Poetry Association (SFPA), and is a past nominee for Best of the Net, and the Rhysling, Elgin, and the Pushcart prizes. In 2024, she was named Laureates' Choice in the Maria W. Faust Sonnet Contest.*

Thief
by Kote Lien

Something sings at me from the cornfields at night. It whispers around the stalks, curling its canines around pale yellow ears, golden. My folks keep saying it's a coyote, to leave well enough alone, but the ones around us don't sound like that. They laugh, they don't sing.

The woman down the road, I tried asking her about it, but she just made the sign of the cross, filled my palms with Werther's hard caramels, gooey and melting through their wrappers, and pushed me out onto her front porch.

I sang back at it, once. Eyes like the setting sun peered out at me, so close I could feel its dew-sweet breath, damp and consuming, fan across my face. My father saw me out there, torches burnt down to embers, nothing on but a sleep shirt and bare feet. He yelled until dawn came round after he got me back inside.

My folks cry in the middle of the night when they think I can't hear them. These walls are plaster-thin and worn with age and I can hear my mother whispering down the phone line, hissing breaths rattling through her frame, as she asks the Pastor what can be done. Her poor, sweet boy has been murdered, she says.

They say their son never had teeth as sharp as mine, eyes quite as calculating as mine. Their son didn't laugh with the coyotes, didn't walk light as crow feathers. In the dark, moonlight peeking in through the slats on the window, I press the tip of my tongue into the crevices of my molars, casting indentations on the fleshy pink muscle.

I don't go outside at night much anymore. Whatever lives in the corn is silent, now.

Kote Lien recently obtained his undergraduate degree in English from the University of Utah. He enjoys spending time with his cat, making costumes and scare-acting in a local haunted house.

Transorbital Aubade
by Julie Allyn Johnson

In a clawfoot tub teeming
with silverfish
I float serene then submerge
beneath its shimmery,
metallic waters.

Unscented candles leap & dance
to the steady drip of a Victorian faucet
widening the blood-brown stain
at the bottom of a cracked, clamshell sink.

A Pied Piper of creep and dank,
the *plunk* and *plink* of every drop
soothes the bristletail gathered here,
seekers that they are
for humid conditions, a moist abode.

Their sleek envelopment cocoons me,
calms my reedy fins, my textured layers,
the throbbing eyeball-ache
of every enlarged appendage.

Pavarotti soars on my Pandora box,
Pachelbel's Canon, a boon
to my fractured psyche.
Medicinal marijuana nearly crosses
the line that separates
the decadent and the existential.

My mind expands beyond the breach.

I feel the squish and wriggle
between every webbed toe,
every oven-warm orifice,
my dawn serenade to M.A.N.,
my nod to its perseverance,
to its streamlined grace.

I yield to the husk and emerge   transformed.

Julie Allyn Johnson is a sawyer's daughter from the American Midwest whose current obsession is tackling the rough and tumble sport of quilting and the accumulation of fabric. A past nominee for the Pushcart Prize and Best of the Net, her poetry can be found in Star*Line, Phantom Kangaroo, Lowestoft Chronicle, Coffin Bell, Chestnut Review, *and other journals. The poem "Transorbital Aubade" previously appeared in* Granfalloon, Fall 2022. *Johnson enjoys photography and writing the occasional haiku, some of which can be found on her blog. Visit: www.asawyersdaughter.com*

Not From Around Here, Are They?

cryptozoological evidence bears witness to wounded queer, reports say
by Liam Strong

it's easier if i disclose what i am up front, easiest if you do the work for both of us to decide for yourself. transparency isn't key, but wants to. i can shift this blood around to give a more convincing presentation. tada. muscle like it's a dying trophy, bonfire of carbs, & it's the year of the rat again. someone's job requires knowing the origins of cobwebs & dust bunnies. you would think i might, but i don't. crickets autotuned with grief ritual. my father tells the neighbors a story surrounding extinguished logs: of me, the first buck, eight point, whose antler had been shot clean off, my spike of putrid velvet. of how pity or generosity become lost or lose themselves in a forest. the result is the same. of course. of how the lesser-known animal must make a name for itself, illusions that magic exists, the moss who etch songs into undergrowth. of hunted things which must remain hunted, or by suggestion, unworthy. fetish of moonless berries, stomach whose pit has no flesh. you're right, correct, even. if i didn't want this attention, i wouldn't identify with targets, their ripples of hypnosis. i won't check for your license, the tags, proof of $5 purchase. there's no one to tell. dying might as well be dying no matter the cause.

Liam Strong (they/them) is a queer neurodivergent cripple punk writer who earned an undergraduate degree writing from University of Wisconsin-Superior. They are the author of the chapbook Everyone's Left the Hometown Show *(Bottlecap Press).* You can find their poetry and essays in Vagabond City, new words {press}, *and other publications. They are almost likely gardening and listening to Bitter Truth somewhere in Northern Michigan. Visit: linktr.ee/liamstrong666*

Far Away Visitor
by Alexander Berkey

October haunting
Cold Van Meter, Iowa
Pumpkins in the fields

Sharp dancing talons
Clicking songs on the rooftops
Batlike wings spread wide

Stench filling the streets
No longer hidden away
Dancing away days

Guns blare at the beast
The visitor sways away
From the killing blows

Alight it fires the
Glowing light upon its brow
At its attackers

Into the dark mines
It was chased by guns and steel
Dancing down mine shafts

Two sets of eyes stare
At dazed terrified hunters
Guns dropped against dirt

Eyes gleam and glitter
As they danced down the coal mine
Never seen again

Alexander Berkey is a new writer on the publishing scene, with graduate school experience in writing academic research articles and fiction. He primarily focuses on horror, fantasy, and historical essays.

Winged
by Brittany Hague

The tent, a cave of whispered secret crushes and stashes of Twin Bing candy wrappers, glowed orange in the light of Jenny's back porch.

I helped put on the birthday gift I gave her. The chain was so thin and delicate, my clumsy fingers struggled with the tiny clasp.

"I love it," she said, rubbing the small pendant between her fingers, the letter "J."

I always fell asleep embarrassingly early at sleepovers and was out before Jenny was. I dreamt that James Vanderbeek slowly unzipped the tent and crawled inside. That sound, like insects—*zzzzzzz*. Metal teeth.

I told the police everything, even that. My cheeks warmed. So stupid, revealing my television crush to a large man in beige. He paused writing on his notepad, but I continued. "Then, he grew wings and took Jenny away," I had stuck my head out from the tent and watched the creature's wings blot out the moon. Jenny dangled from its arms. But it was a dream. I told him. That's all.

But that wasn't all; Jenny was gone. That was no dream.

You're traumatized, mixing it all up with silly local legends, they said. My little brother apologized, he was the one who told me about the winged man, had seen it outside his window. Jenny's family couldn't look at me, sure I was suppressing something that would save her. There had been other missing girls, after all.

The warm autumn air froze, yellows turned white. Hope of finding her faded. It was then that the technician repairing telephone lines found them. About fifty in all, pieces of jewelry glittering in the halo of the Iowan winter sun. Silver tennis bracelets, a worn and woven friendship bracelet, and a delicate chain of gold, the letter "J."

Brittany Hague (she/her) is a Seattle-based graphic artist and short-story writer. Her work has appeared in the anthologies Night of the Geminids *and* Monster *from Hidden Fortress Press, as well as* Last Girls Club, Willows Wept Review, Saw Palm, *and* Bog Fancy. *She is a graduate of film and video program at The Rhode Island School of Design.*

The Rhinelander Hodag
by Sean Glatch

The Rhinelander Hodag drives my car
down Capitol Road, street lights silvering
the gleam of his teeth. I could smell the asphalt
simmering in his cheeks—asked him to fill
my mouth with brimstone—lips magnetized
to the heat of his lips as his spine
molts to spikes. No—we never kissed,
but our tongues came close to touching
and I smelled the salt of his pits. Sunk
in the warmth of his fleece, I wouldn't shower
for weeks. The Hodag was all teeth, no terror—
except when I realized I wanted him to eat me,
my flesh a sacrament, or a toll you pay
to cross a river. His spiked thighs pressed
into me like thorns in rotted fruit,
a blackberry pricked on its bush.
He spoke in tales so told they're prehistoric,
but I would have loved him in the Cenozoic
if it weren't for the glow of the stoplights
sweating the myth from the monster—no—
I could have loved him. Even as a man.

*Sean Glatch is a queer poet, storyteller, and screenwriter in New York City.
His work has appeared in* Ninth Letter, Milk Press, 8Poems, The Poetry
Annals, *on television, and elsewhere. Sean currently runs Writers.com, the
oldest writing school on the internet. When he's not writing, which is often,
he thinks he should be writing. Visit: seanglatch.com*

One New Follower
by Stuart Conover

Tasha left work late, her boots clicking against the damp pavement.
Chicago's skyline shimmered in the river's reflection. She flipped open
    her front camera, tilting her chin just right.
Snap.
She loved that her phone sounded like an actual camera when she took
    a selfie.
She kept walking, scrolling through her phone.
Ignoring the people around her.
Habit.
Distraction.
She posted her selfie.
Then her stomach dropped.
The photo was—wrong.
Her face was fine.
Lipstick still on point, hair curled from the mist.
But something perched on the lamppost across the street behind her.
It was winged, but it wasn't a bird. It was tall, humanoid,
    and had red eyes.
Her breath hitched.
How had she missed it?
Tasha's phone buzzed from a new notification.
One new follower.
Her fingers shook as she swiped to see who it was.
No username.
No account.
Just red eyes staring from the shadows of a tiny profile circle.
A gust of wind rustled the river's edge.
The street, teeming moments ago, was now seemingly empty.
But she wasn't alone.
She looked up.

The lampposts were bare.
Yet she knew she was being watched.

Stuart Conover is a father, husband, rescue dog owner, horror author and enthusiast, blogger, journalist, comic book geek, science-fiction junkie, fantasy fanatic, and information technology professional. With all of that, he rarely sleeps and relies on caffeine to get through most days. He currently resides in the suburbs of Chicago with his family.

My Child Asks What the Consequence Is ...
by Katie King

For the Cheese-Fed Midwest Monster Man,
who jumps out of the moving car on the way to Sin City,
I show you the inside of a burrito.

Layered with cotton candy,
larger than your thigh,
candle-lit and sparkling,
pumped with Thai tea ice cream,
and three dry toppings that I wish were wet.

I show you the bright lights of Vegas.
This city is corrupt, they say,
and I sit in the convenience of distracting.
Corruption with CORRUPTION.
A gold tooth for a Golden Nugget.

I show you the neon signs,
the way the glass milky-swooped and swirled to say Moulin Rouge,
the homesky color of the glass,
the powder inside the Argan Green waving.

I hand you a matchbox from a man
who said his soul was draining out of his asshole,
and tell you to press firmly and swipe right to make a flame.

Oh, how the cleaning chemicals wreaked threats.

LOOK HERE
DON'T LOOK HERE
NOTHING TO SEE HERE

I show you the cold temperature of the Yeti,
served in an ice bar at the Venetia,
and the bartender saying asshole and I'm sorry, I'm sorry.

The cover of a book with the same name
(I'm Sorry, I'm Sorry, I'm Sorry),
and a giant sleeping rabbit
who was complete in his anti-glitz and glam giantry.

I didn't show you another book about Lucille Ball,
you chose that one on your own.

I don't show you the naked women
on the cards scattered,
but you see them anyway.
You mention those women don't have rosacea like I do.
A donkey-arse covered in tights and feathered fanfare.

I ask where the naked men are.
Society's ongoing scavenger hunt that can never be found.
Look for the naked men,
and wonder why they are always buying but never being sold.

I direct you toward the fountain,
towards heights higher than heels,
higher and more beautiful things—
the perfect segue for a mother to speak of cheap thrills,
like easy answers and easy ways out,
and the terrible artistry in things that take time.

Like sitting with your feelings in a car
and keeping the door—and your mouth—shut.

I say: I bet you have a question for every single fountain,
and I show you how the answers
dissolved like mist.

I show you how it all didn't destroy me and I was fine.
(Which was arguably more destructive.)

I took your picture over and over again
so that all you'd reflect on was the flash of light itself,
blinding you from me.

Oil paintings found in a converted vending machine.
Things that almost looked as they are.
A red door, an accompanying cactus.
How quickly the oil seemed to matter.

How much I loved oil,
and wanted to feel it rushing around on my fingers,
how much more worthy it seemed than watercolor,
my grandfather's medium.

Water could wash away, away,
but oil had danger to it,
a permeating glaze.

I let you choose a slot machine and we watch.
The Cheese-Fed Midwest Monster Man gambles on the metal box of
your choice,
which got you fifty-seven cents.
But just printed on a receipt.

I let you inhale smoke till you coughed,
and then said, I think we need to get out of here.

I show you the cold red LOVE letters,
and tell you to raise your arms up
above to match the slant in the V
because your name has one in it,
but your arms are little
and instead of cold brass metal, soft.

I spit black in the sink because of the Pepto Bismol.
That same Cheese-Fed Midwest Monster Man had stayed up with me all
night long
making sure I was okay,
and then every few months,
making sure I wasn't.

And oh, when you quietly asked if you may have bipolar too,
I showed you what saying I don't know sounds like
on the tongue of a mother
who always wanted you to come
to your own conclusions.

For that sad weekend, we lived
on Italian Cookie ice cream and Frank Sinatra.

When you called me a liar,
I showed you how much your words hurt
my caramel onion-string feelings.

And ugh, when the Cheese-Fed Midwest Monster Man came into the
bathroom, telling us our water heater was making a noise, I told you to
HURRY
and slathered conditioner on your hair
as you gasped in the cold water,
forgetting to tell you
you were brave for breathing.

I showed you a chicken ramen soup we shared—
so good it could have knelt to your grandmothers'.

Rust-colored oil ruining my white outfit,
I take the orangey splattered Styrofoam with me in the car,
and the Cheese-Fed Midwest Monster Man said That won't work–it
will go bad in the heat. He's right. But I did it anyway,
because I want her close to me.

I wonder what take-out box will house me
by your shoes one day as you stumble,
which odorous flavor, chock full of stringed chicken.

I showed you how patience and a smile can get your glasses back
from the Venetian when dropped in the water,
the price tag on Armani shoes,
and how some things hold different amounts of meaning
depending on what we carry.

On the road home, I complained
that nobody said Happy 35th Birthday to me.
When we got home, I threw the sheet over you
again and again,
like a tablecloth master till my arms hurt,
while you curled up and smiled.

I told you that if you got through the summer without being angry,
I'd give you $400,
even though you knew there was no way I could afford that,
but I could afford, for a moment,
the belief in miracles never to occur.

How you can see the stars here,

but we never look for him,
almost a defiant avoidance at this point.

Star-blind, with it all laid out for us in the open.

The Cheese-Fed Midwest Monster Man was afraid of heights.
So you wanted him to take the Ferris wheel as a consequence—
to feel fear the way he made us feel it.
But we wouldn't sink that low
just to reach those heights.
Instead, we stayed home.
We stayed home for a long time.

How you said,
YOU AREN'T TREVOR NOAH'S MOTHER.
THIS ISN'T A THIRD-WORLD COUNTRY.
NO ONE IS CHASING US.

How the right way to be
sticks to you
like danger.

Katie King is a second-soprano who always wanted to be an alto. Wearing blue suede heels to breakfast, she finds herself allergic to the banana. She lives at high altitudes telling middle-brow jokes to her second-grader, who often tells her to get real. The lady doth wish she had happy love stories to write. Still, only pain itself drifts to her doorstep. Visit: cargocollective.com/katieking

Woman dreaming winter away in the Michigan U.P.
by Callie S. Blackstone

Dogman: 7 feet tall.
The legends tell of blue or golden
eyes—take your pick. They burn
with hunger either way.
He lurks in the woods,
only leaves to lunge after
his prey–she imagines
his desire for her pale
thighs, her body flushes
with the thought. She welcomes
the heat, imagines the feel
of his furry torso—dark brown
or black, your pick—under
her hands, her mouth.
The way his howl
would split open the cold, dark
night. And when she is done
dreaming, her body blazing hot
against the winter, she claps
loudly, striking the flesh
of her palms together to scare off
the monster. That's what the legends
say to do, anyway.

Callie S. Blackstone writes both poetry and prose. She has been nominated for a Pushcart and Best of the Net. Her debut chapbook sing eternal *is available through Bottlecap Press. Visit: calliesblackstone.com*

The Ohio Grassman
by David Clink

A tree stands in a henge of many trees,
hearing bark cracking, numerous,

petroglyphs on cave walls, campfires,
journeys, invasive plants, the death of reason.

The Northern Lights are for all of us—

you intuit from the Ohio Grassman, as it
once stood taller than the sugar maple, before

it receded into the night, for good, for always.
Cirrus giving way. Stars parting.

Brown bears standing still.

David Clink's poem "A sea monster tells his story" won the 2013 Aurora Award for Best Poem/Song. Clink's latest collection is The Black Ship *(Aeolus House). Visit: davidlivingstoneclink.com*

The Ozark Howler
by Scott Chaddon

A thin figure wearing a gray, prison uniform sprinted through the trees, scattering small animals in every direction. The crimson-colored sky warned him that nightfall was near. Ray Brunt could hear the hounds and guards closing in as he fled from the Ozark Correctional Facility. He had killed two guards during his escape, and they were out for blood. But if he could reach the Arkansas border, freedom would be his.

The hounds stopped at the tree line, refusing to enter the forest. Corrections Officer Blake called to advise Warden O'Connell of the situation. The Warden radioed back a simple, "Understood." He knew that the dogs would not track when the Ozark Howler was on the hunt. He almost pitied Brunt. Almost.

After a while, the hounds' baying faded, before ceasing altogether. Ray paused and, after several minutes of silence, was convinced that he was no longer being pursued. Brunt wondered why the hunt had ended. As the last remnant sunlight faded away, he decided that it did not matter, Arkansas awaited.

As he took his first step, a loud, unearthly cry made him freeze. It sounded like a mingling of a wolf's howl and elk's bugle. The disturbing call made Ray's blood run cold and brought to mind the rumors about these woods. The next howl sounded far too close for comfort, so Brunt turned and fled. After 20 minutes of running, as the howls grew closer, he was stopped in his tracks as a huge creature leapt at him. It had long, black fur, red, glowing eyes, and a wolf-like head sporting two, long, curved horns. Before he could react, the monster was upon him. It was unimaginably fast and, as Ray felt the claws tear into him, he knew that he would never reach Arkansas.

Scott Chaddon was born, raised, and educated in Fairbanks, Alaska before it started to warm up. Reading, art, winter sports, and tabletop role-playing games were common means of escaping the harsh winter weather. He eventually became interested in creative writing, particularly horror, fantasy, and science fiction. He has been published in several anthologies and magazines, and enjoys sharing his ideas, stories, and worlds with others.

It's Not Easy Being Green
by Bill Bibo Jr.

A slight tremor ran down the hodag's thick spiked vertebrae and along its tail. It flexed dangerously long talons as it stared at the overstuffed leather couch. "Do you expect me to climb up there?"

"Only if you want to. It's been reinforced to assist other clients, but actually, it's not very comfortable anymore. There is an area in the corner that might be more suitable." The bespectacled therapist pointed to a rust-colored section of deep shag carpet.

The creature lumbered to the spot, circled once and hooked the lampshade with its bowed horns, bringing it crashing to the ground. "Sorry about that."

"I'll just add it to your bill. Now then, what brings you to see me today?"

The hodag let loose a foul, smokey sigh. "Doctor, do you see me?"

The psychiatrist nodded and scribbled in her notepad. "Of course."

"Good. Lately, I've been doubting my existence."

"How so? You seem as real as I am."

"I'm from the Wisconsin north woods. If you go there, you'll see images of me everywhere. Businesses use it in their logos. The local high school has me as their mascot, though no one asked me. There's even a life-sized statue in front the Chamber of Commerce. It's not very flattering."

"That all seems very nice."

"It might be, except no one believes I actually exist. They all think I'm made up, a hoax created by some prankster that just caught on."

The psychiatrist scribbled some more. "You seem to be having what is called an existential crisis. To combat these feelings, you must find meaning in your life."

"How do I do that?"

"That's something we can work on next week."

Sitting in the waiting room, a jackalope checked his watch when the door opened and no one came out.

Bill Bibo Jr. was raised in Peoria, Illinois, but escaped after college and has enjoyed life in Madison, Wisconsin for more than 40 years. He is currently putting the finishing touches on a quirky urban fantasy mystery about a detective team of the reanimated mummy of Ramses II and a newly created golem—the work was recently named as a Claymore Award finalist for best unpublished mystery fiction. His stories can be found in such venues as Stupefying Stories, Havok, Timeless Tales, Black Ink Fiction, Black Hare Press, *and many others. Visit: billbibojr.com*

My father tells me about life in the Michigan U.P.
by Callie S. Blackstone

Every story starts like this: what you have to understand
is that the winters were bleak. Total darkness, total cold,
total snow. The trailer didn't hold heat. My mother wouldn't hold
money. Every winter, all I had was sneakers, duck-taped
so they wouldn't fall apart. No snow boots here.
It's a miracle I have all of my toes. Dark, cold, snow.
No money. What was there to do? Where did all the money go?
Well, booze and drugs of course. There isn't anything to do out there
otherwise, even if you do have money. Beer, weed, shrooms,
even a line now and then if I could get it. I didn't use it often,
it always made me antsy and hungry for more. But yeah,
that's what it was like for your old man back in the day.
Adopted mother an alcoholic and drinking the only family
bonding we ever did. It was the seventies.
Everyone smoked weed. Stop rolling
your eyes. I'm your father. If I want to tell you
the same old story, I'll tell it to you as many times
as I want. You're lucky, you've got boots and food.
You've got more than I did. But anyway, kid, I'm telling you
this for a reason–I always do. You see, everyone up that way
makes a life of drinking and getting high. So when your uncle called
and told you about the GIANT GREEN SQUIRREL
        that he heard about
over in that tiny town, well, kid, they're all drunk as a skunk
and feeding into each other's stupidity. GIANT GREEN SQUIRREL
my ass. Ain't no squirrel as big as a '72 Buick. They can't even get
the color of his eyes right, that always changes depending on
        who's telling it.

I mean really. Do you really believe in a GIANT GREEN SQUIRREL
that only comes out at night and terrorizes people
with his chirping? Do you even know
what a squirrel sounds like? You're a city kid.
You don't get it. What did we move here for?
I thought the schools here were better
and here you are talking
about a GIANT GREEN SQUIRREL.
Now Bigfoot? That's a different story.

*Callie S. Blackstone writes both poetry and prose. She has been nominated
for a Pushcart and Best of the Net. Her debut chapbook* sing eternal *is
available through Bottlecap Press. Visit: calliesblackstone.com*

A Night and a Day on the Big Onion
by Herb Kauderer

Long ago I got to work for Paul Bunyan when he was logging Michigan near the Big Onion River. Bunyan had plenty of lumberjacks—what they really needed was paperpushers, he explained.

Bjorn with the mustache laughed at me when he heard that my job was to count the logged trees. I asked him what the joke was.

"Last winter in South Dakota we logged 246 million feet of timber, and we've expanded. There isn't no way you can count all that by yerself."

There was only one reasonable course of action to being laughed at, so I bet Bjorn that in the next 48 hours I could count all the timber logged so far. That gave him another good laugh. We got a witness, wagered a year's salary, and he kept laughing.

Now Paul was not the full 63 axe-handles-tall as the legends say. Really, he was no more than 59 axe-handles top to bottom. Those of you who study artistic anatomy will know that Paul's hat had to be taller than me. So I spent that night sewing a perch onto the back of it.

When Paul rose for the day, I greeted him, and explained my plan. As Paul and his pet ox checked in on his crews, I sat in my perch at the back of his hat with a spyglass and a ledger, making my counts.

At the end of being up all night, and working hard all day, dinner never tasted better. Especially with all of Bjorn's money in my pocket. I had thought he'd try to welch, but it turns out people west of Lake Michigan are pretty much always good to their word. In the morning I shook Bjorn's hand and retired from my career as a timber counter.

Herb Kauderer is a tenured English professor at Hilbert College south of Buffalo, New York. His writing has won the Asimov's Science Fiction Magazine *Readers' Award,* The Critter's *Readers' Award, and other*

accolades. He has written for film and stage, fiction, non-fiction, and a ridiculous amount of poetry. One of his hobbies is walking the eastern shore of Lake Erie stealing poetry from seagulls only to lose it in the wind. Visit: www.HerbKauderer.com

The Sasquatchian Blue Beast of the Ozarks
by Kevin Novalina

"It is a genuine Ozark legend, and if the testimony during all these years is to be accepted, the legend is absolutely true."
—Springfield Leader, 1924

Misty morning pelts the face
of my fight through mountain wilds
beyond the pale, tracking beast-prints
swollen with rain. I halt
at every limb snap and bracken crack,
nostrils flexing for an odor
more foul than skunk spray
as the cavern's guttural winds growl
against extinction. Starved to feed
my need to know, I search for the first
of the last
of its kind,
eyes craving what is said I've never seen,

that twisted myth of Mother and Man,
reason and rage, posture and primal instinct.

Such imagination, they say,
to flesh a thicket with dark fur
made blue by light and berries,
or raise a deadfall upright,
skull ridged in an ape's sagittal crest,
taller than man with man-legs
and a mother's udders
swinging with its long stride
like cradled young at suckle,

to have it slip all vegetation
with bipedal grace and cryptid stealth,
to find its human eyes in bestial stare,
finding me, finding me.

Kevin Novalina has published three short-story collections, including Death Roll *(Lame Goat Press)* and Ink On Wood *(Virgogray Press). The Arkansas-based writer's fiction, non-fiction, and poetry has appeared in more than 200 journals, magazines, and anthologies. He has been nominated for a Pushcart Prize four times. Visit: www.kevinnovalina.com*

A Giant Misunderstanding
by Richard Lau

Dear Paul,

We Midwesterners have a reputation for being somewhat naïve, simple folks, but your recent antics on the Internet are giving us a bad name. So, in the spirit of community kindness, I'd like to offer the following tips for posting on-line.

First, do not type in ALL CAPS. For a newbie, this might seem like a good way to get attention. However, it is the equivalent of rudely shouting in someone's ear. Also, proper capitalization can eliminate some possible confusion.

Second, try to be as clear as possible. Remember, most likely you won't be present when the reader is trying to decipher your words.

Third, make certain you are posting to the correct message board. DO NOT (all caps used intentionally for emphasis) post ads for a missing pet to a dating site!

As a free-spirited, confidant, single young woman who appreciates directness and honesty, you can understand my misunderstanding when reading:

"BIG MAN SEEKING HORNY HOT BABE"

As I mentioned in my profile, being tall, I am only interested in dating men over 6-feet-tall. So, naturally, I thought we were a good match.

Nevertheless, once I properly understood the situation, I was happy to help find your giant blue ox with the big horns before it got too overheated and dehydrated from the unusually warm Michigan summer we are experiencing.

Now, if you could explain to my insurance company how my truck got flattened by a humongous hoof, I'd be much obliged.

I'll need transportation for I have found a more compatible match. He's a Mac OS guy who is witty and flirty.

"Apple-loving Johnny seeks travel companion to help spread his seed."

No more misunderstandings here!

Moving on from fairy tales,
Hannah

Richard Lau is an award-winning writer who is published in magazines, newspapers, and anthologies, as well as in industry and on-line. His stories have recently appeared in Carpe Noctem *(Tyche Books) and* Sinister Century: Capture *(Disturb Ink Books). Visit: www.isfdb.org/cgi-bin/ea.cgi?289945*

The Unseen Surge
by Alexandra "Sasha" Shandrenko

We are the pulse of the earth,
beneath the surface,
quietly gathering,
until the moment is ripe.
Individually, we are small,
just a flicker in the vastness—
but together,
we are a surge,
a wave that will crash,
and leave no stone unturned.
We rise from the cracks,
the voices once unheard,
now shaking the foundations
of everything that stood in our way.
The torrent grows,
with each word that escapes our lips,
with each injustice we name,
we reshape the world—
a new landscape formed by the flood
of voices that refuse to stay silent.

Alexandra Shandrenko is a federal Information Technologies auditor with a passion for storytelling. Balancing the precision of her technical work with the creativity of writing, she explores themes of identity, resilience, and human connection through poetry and prose. When she's not auditing systems, she's crafting narratives that resonate, challenge, and inspire. Visit: www.linkedin.com/in/alexandra-shandrenko-799640236

Squonks, Squawks, & Sirens

Wisconsin Giants Emerging, Darkness
by David Clink

Upon a table, dissected—
it had a blue whale's heart, the coroner
describing it as a house with many rooms
with a gazebo in the back

and a hedge grown large
through generations, a pair
of fully-inflated horse lungs
and a vocabulary of discrete symbols.

Somewhere, in all of this, there is
a scientific explanation for ghosts,
the gene for language,
hominid evolution.

The dinosaurs learned about fire
the hard way. They had become
too big, their knowledge of fire
passed down to birds.

We are giants to our ancestors,
walking in their shadows,
dinosaur bones speaking,
voices rising from the darkness.

David Clink's poem "A sea monster tells his story" won the 2013 Aurora Award for Best Poem/Song. Clink's latest collection is The Black Ship *(Aeolus House). Visit: davidlivingstoneclink.com*

Bigfoot Farewell
by Carolyn Clink

I wove my fur moults
into throw rugs,
my manifestos
papered the pine walls,
but I was alone.

Time to shed my form,
dim these glowing eyes,
become something else –
perhaps a Great Lakes mermaid
or a *Mishipeshu*.

Dank, hairy, pungent—
I'll gladly leave that behind.
As I metamorphose,
snow turns the forest black
and white and silent.

Carolyn Clink has had poems published in numerous magazines and anthologies over the past 40 years. She is a member of the Science Fiction and Fantasy Poetry Association (SFPA). She has had a soft spot for Bigfoot ever since meeting him in the 1960s at Girl Scout camp. But that is a story for another day. Visit: sfwriter.com/carolyn.htm

The Lake Bottom
by Leah Fletcher

"Don't you dare tip me over." The Girl's authoritative tone was undermined by panic. She moved crab-like from the dock onto the inner tube, with only her bottom exposed to the cold water.

The Boy lowered himself into the water slowly, trying not to make waves. His toes squidged into the mucky Lake Bottom and it felt wrong, like standing on a decaying corpse. He carefully pushed his floating sister through the weeds. It was the price he paid for being the younger sibling—braving the Lake Bottom so she wouldn't have to.

The Lake Bottom stirred. It wasn't The Boy's tentative footsteps on her expansive abdomen that roused her. It was the panic in The Girl's tone. She needed The Girl to know who The Lake Bottom really was: not muck, but all of life's fallen treasure—silver scales, emerald flies, and garnet leaves—given over to her for Processing.

The Boy had almost gotten past the weeds when one wrapped itself around his ankle. "Ah! The seaweed's got me!" He grabbed onto the inner tube.

"Let go!" The Girl peeled his fingers off one by one. "You're going to tip me. And anyway, it's not seaweed, you dummy. It's a lake. It's just plants."

The Lake Bottom sniffed at the scent of heightened panic. Just one more push.

The Boy felt a tickle on the bottom of his foot and squealed out of the water onto one side of the tube, upsetting the balance.

The Girl toppled in. The Boy reached out to his sister, but all he could see was a tangle of weeds and muck-stirred water.

The Lake Bottom embraced her new object, holding tight until the thrashing stopped so the Processing could begin.

Leah Fletcher is a proud native of Minnesota, where the lake bottom always creeped her out. She now lives with her family in North Yorkshire, where she enjoys sharing a cup of tea and a good story with her writing group, Write-On Ripon. Visit: stillpeaking.substack.com

Cry Me a Squonk
by Avalon Rain Anderson

I am only a Squonk
I cry for hours
My eyes grow red and sour
The tears pour down my cheeks
Like a swamp that calls
My voice creaks
My throat raw
My thoughts scream
At nothing at all
The kindness of touch
Can be ever cruel
For what truly I yearn
Is never at my fall
My face a mess
My skin with warts
My body sags
With these harsh words
The distaste I see
On all the faces
Time may pass
But the scars never may
So what else can I do
But weep at my loss
Melt in my ways
And water the crops
Ridding the world
Of my horrid taste
So I may dampen the ground
And grew something new
Something that's proud

Something so overdue
Maybe then I will be a beautiful thing
And be in the crowd

Avalon Anderson is a recent graduate from California State Polytechnic University in Pomona, getting her degree in agriculture. She has been writing and doing photography since high school, and has an innate curiosity for anything weird and spooky.

The Loveland Frogman
by Mia Dalia

To get love in Loveland one has to fit in.
It won't do to have webbed feet, gills, or fins.
It's a heartbreaking truth and a terrible thing,
and I hide for the fear of being seen.

If you're built like a man but you look like a frog,
if you're caught in the headlights, crossing the road,
better run lest you caught, better scamper away,
make them think you're an iguana without a tail.

There's a certain infamy I inspire
in a small town of Loveland, Ohio.
But close your eyes, I'll have you convinced.
Kiss me, darling, I'm a proper frog prince.

Mia Dalia's tales of horror, noir, science fiction, mystery, crime, humor, and more have been featured in a variety of anthologies, magazines, literary journals, on-line, and adapted for narrative podcasts. Her stories were voted top ten of Tales to Terrify 2023, acclaimed by Booklist, and shortlisted for the Crime Writers Association's 2024 Daggers Awards. She's the author of novels Estate Sale *and* Haven; *the novellas* Alakazam, Tell Me a Story, Discordant, Arrokoth, *and* Do You Know The Muffin Man?; *and the short-story collection* Smile So Red and Other Tales of Madness. *Visit:* daliaverse.wixsite.com/author

Little Lost Lake Monster
by Liam Espinoza-Zemlicka

Donna locked eyes with the head sticking out of the water.

"That's Champ right?" Peggy asked, flicking her eyes between Donna and the animal.

It had a sort of pointed head, like a Roman spear tip, with eyes on either side and a long neck that remained stationary even as the ripples in the lake indicated its body was moving.

"Which one's Champ?" David's voice went low.

"Lake Champlain," Donna said, stepped forward slowly. "She is way out of her way. God look at her. She's not a fish or really an aquatic mammal either."

David caught Peggy's eye. "The hell's going on with her?"

Donna made a swatting at David's direction. "Nothing" she said, her voice level. "We're face to face with something that defies categorization, forgive a little awe."

"Okay," David said, keeping his tranquilizer rifle poised, "but what's it doing all the way out here? I mean ... it's a Northeastern Cryptid and we're in Illinois. It couldn't have swum here."

"Doctor Sharma say they're not prone to wandering so ..." Peggy scanned the trees that lined the shore. "I only see one real possibility."

"You think someone put it here?"

"Her" Donna said. She reached her hand out and Champ bowed her head. Donna brushed her fingers against the top of the animal's head.

"Her ... Robbins if this turns into a 'Shape of Water' thing, I'm requesting a transfer."

"Shut up," Donna said, voice still calm.

It donned on Peggy what she was doing, measuring her tone to keep Champ calm. Robbins wasn't some military grunt recruited because she was good with guns. She had a way with animals—a sense for them.

"Radio headquarters—tell them to bring whatever it is we carry one of her in. Keep scanning the trees. Someone put her here and they might've lingered."

Liam Espinoza-Zemlicka is a writer, teacher, and scholar from Southern California. His fiction has previously been published in Grim and Gilded *and* Uncharted Magazine, *where he was a winner of a 2023 Novel Excerpt Prize. His writing explores mysteries, legends, and the place that the supernatural holds in our everyday live as well as good old-fashioned pulp adventure. As a scholar, he studies the place of race and identity in pop culture fandom.*

Frogmen at the Loveland Castle, Ohio
by Lora Butcher

Secrets in shadows, the frogs in the river,
as big as big dogs, make grown men quiver,
because they're unknown, uncharted, unmeasured,
police have shot at them before they're treasured.

Knights of the Golden Trail have discovered them
down at the river, getting rocks at the rim
of the known and the unknown of all of life,
the stones that build a castle sharpen a knife.

The frogmen have learned all they need to know
from the modern knights in time's gentle flow,
men as surprising as frogs four feet tall,
have invited the frogs to a nighttime ball.

Joy by the river, they sung and they danced;
one by one, they gave each other a chance,
the shadows of night, the halos of fire
played over their bodies, lower and higher.

Strange monsters they made by the shades of themselves,
By water and stone, together they delved
past limits of being what nature revealed
to depths of the soul and promises sealed

through decades of wonder and thrill at the keep
of friendship together that rose from the deep
waters that thundered and roared on the way
to clearing assumptions that cluttered the day.

When the party was done, they leapt off the stone
back to the river, to stay mostly unknown,
the frogmen of Loveland, monsters of legend,
who knights of the castle had turned into friends.

Lora Butcher was moderator of a 200,000-member Disqus channel called "Poetry Park." She has been published in The Lyric, Time Of Singing, Ink to Paper Vol. 8 & 9, 100 Poems of Hope Anthology, *and* The Heartland Review. *She won Carmel Creative Writers Tanka contest. She won second place in the 2023 Linda Bannon Memorial contest, and second place in the 2024 Bright Star Award of the Poetry Society of Indiana.*

Another Miracle
by Dane Erbach

Flung over his jet-ski's handlebars, Troy splashed into the Fox River's chocolate-milky murk. He retched as he surfaced, gagging on the humid fall air and shaking clumps of hair out of his eyes.

On the shore, the party pulsated like a distant dream. Music echoed between the riverbanks as his friends chugged Old Style along with the last dregs of summer in board shorts and bikinis.

"What the ..." he burped, wondering what he hit. As he swam closer to the bobbing jet-ski, the river's bottom rose beneath his knees only inches beneath the surface. A sandbar? he thought, except it felt hard, slick, like mossy layers of prehistoric slate.

Troy climbed to his feet. From the shore, it must have looked like he was walking on water. "Hey!" he yelled, catching his friends' attention. "Check this out!" Their phones flashed in the copper sun, so Troy struck a surfer pose. They squealed, hoisted their cans high.

Somehow, Troy discovered, he had drifted 20 feet downriver from his jet-ski. Just the current, he told himself. As he splashed upriver, holding out his hands like some savior performing a miracle, his friends exploded. "Jesus walks!" Brody roared.

Troy grinned, dashed downriver like one of those insane lizards, kicking up brown plumes of water. He heard mad howls from the shore until he dropped off some ledge and crashed into the Fox River's full depths.

The enormous river worm on which Troy had tread drew him into its puckered mouth before he could comprehend what happened. He drowned there silently, peacefully, providing much-needed nourishment to the ancient monster migrating south for the season.

But, on the shore, Brody's phone only recorded Troy's sudden disappearance, not the worm maneuvering beneath the surface. "And he's gone!" he announced before realizing something was wrong, "Another miracle!"

Dane Erbach is a writer from Chicago's northwest suburbs who teaches English and journalism at a public high school. His writing has appeared in Mythaxis Magazine, Perseid Prophecies, *the Frightening Tales podcast,* JMWW Journal, *and elsewhere. His novel* Friday Night at Humble House *was published in 2024. When not writing or reading, you can find him catching Pokémon with his family, raiding his community library, and tending to the pumpkin patch in his backyard. Visit: daneerbach.com.*

Godzilla at the Pow Wow
by Juan Manuel Pérez

drumbeat, drumbeat, drum
a deep rhythmic rumbling sound
music from the heart

he shows up sometimes
after messing up a place
to cool himself off

drumbeat, drumbeat, drum
back since the Astro-Monster
dancing for the win

dancing for his life
dancing for it is sacred
dancing for prayer

drumbeat, drumbeat, drum
he must be part NDN
puts him in a trance

pow wows aren't the same
without a kaiju stomp dance
peyote puff clouds

drumbeat, drumbeat, drum
reminds him of something gone
he never says what

Juan Manuel Pérez, a Mexican-American poet of Indigenous descent and the Poet Laureate for Corpus Christi, Texas (2019-2020), is the author of more than 15 poetry collections, including Screw The Wall! And Other Brown People Poems (2020), Planet Of The Zombie Zonnets: Seasons One And Two (2021), *and* Thirty Years Ago: Life and the First Gulf War (2023). *He is a former Gourd Dancer for the Memphis Tia Piah Big River Clan Warrior Society is as well as a SEATTAH Scholar (Striving For Excellence And Accountability In The Teaching Of Traditional American History) through the University of Dallas. Pérez is a 10-year Navy Corpsman/Combat Marine Medic, with experiences in the 1991 Persian Gulf War (Operations Desert Shield, Desert Storm, and Desert Calm), as well as other missions. Visit: www.juanmperez.com*

Centennial Bridge
by Lumina Miller

My thoughts scratch and whisper after a respite of unconscious hours. Millenia old flashes from when I could walk along the beach, as well as swim, color me with calm. When the eastern sky begins to blush, I can remember what hope tasted like. Then I look down at my scales, realize I have six heads and growl—setting the water to rumble.

There are pounds of resentment within me. Mainly towards the sorceress, but at Glaucos too. I'm repulsive and eternally pissed off because I turned a guy down. I used to decimate ships and eat the crew, reveling in a trance of revenge.

A young man with a green hat changed that. He was perched on a rock observing the horizon with exquisite toffee-colored-eyes and curiosity. Instead of racing through the water to strike, I sank down and held my breath to get closer. His pocket began buzzing and then he spoke.

"I'll be back at the Davenport plant on Thursday, yeah. Take the 50-cent bridge, it's faster." He stood up, looked in my direction and jumped down to the beach.

My chest became a balmy swell as he walked away. The temptation to tap into the anger Circe planted contracted making room for warmth. I followed cargo ships and barges with the image that was on his hat. Whirling through atypical waters far from the familiar swirl and spray has whittled down the penchant for vengeance. It's good to be away from the tours that discuss my demise. I let go of killing for a pastime—but I'm not wholly good. A girl's got to eat.

The Mississippi River is noiseless compared to the Straits. It's been years since I first saw him, but I made it to Davenport, Iowa. I believe I'll find John Deere.

Lumina Miller has an undergraduate degree in English from the University of Iowa. She enjoys letting her imagination run wild. Her work has been published in by literary magazines Black Mountain Press, The Write Launch, Drunk Monkeys *and others.*

Pepie
by Topher Nelson

On a lake of ice beneath a concrete sky
A tiny shack like a tombstone lies.
Within the shack of wood and nail
An old man sits upon an upturned pail.
In gloved hands he holds a rod
As a radio preaches the word of God.
The line's been still all the day
Like all the walleye had just run away.
But to catch a fish isn't the goal
Of dropping a line into the hole.
It's a meditation, retreat, a time to think
A time to be quiet, a time to drink.
And this fisherman's had a few
But for this old man that's nothing new.
Shaken from his stupor by a tug on the line
He grumbles to himself, "It's about damn time."
He cranks the reel and the line goes taut
A flash of excitement wondering what he's caught.
Too deep for a bluegill, too strong for a pike
But he knows that it's big, based on the strike.
He reels it in slow, taking his time
Being sure not to put too much stress on the line.
Then without warning the line goes slack; The ice under his feet
    starts to crack.
Lake water gushing from the icy hole
Numbing his body and freezing his soul.
Beneath his feet the ground starts to swell
And from the ice bursts a creature of hell.
The old man scrambles to get out from beneath
Its serpentine neck and mouth full of teeth.

Its coal black eyes stare and look down
To where the angler lies shaking on the ground.
A terrible cry and then the ice quakes
Then cold silence settles on the lake.
The angler learned a rod's no weapon
To catch Pepie, the serpent of Lake Pepin.

Topher Nelson graduated from Iowa State University in 1997, and taught high school English in the bush of Alaska and in northwest Iowa after graduating. He moved to Minnesota in 2006, and taught in the private sector for 16 years before a degenerative disease forced an early retirement. Since then, he has rediscovered his love of poetry and table-top role-playing games, and has started to use each as a creative outlet.

Middle Management
by Paul Cesarini

This was confusing, thought Ari-6, the control panel lights reflecting off its domed head in the otherwise dark room. The High-Speed Aerial Assault Vertical Take-off units, or HSAAVTs, essentially had the same acronym as the High-Velocity Armored Assault Strategic Tactical units, or HVAASTs. When given orders to launch the HSAAVT phalanx just now, how could it be sure beyond any reasonable doubt that the orders actually meant what they said? What if the orders were actually to launch the HVAAST phalanx instead? That would involve entirely different protocols and command codes.

Executing the first order typically took between 1.2 to 2.63 cycles. The second took twice that—on a good day—assuming all weather conditions were optimal and each unit was fully charged. If, however, those two letters were inadvertently transposed, the first phalanx would require 72 percent of the munitions resources needed by the correct, actual units. Once the mistake was discovered, it would take another 3.52 cycles to remove the munitions from the HSAAVT units, transport them to their HVAAST brethren, then reload each unit.

It could shave off a third of that time by routing the incorrect group backward through the munitions assembly depot. That would assume that each unit was at least a model 3 or 4. They were supposed to be model year 6 or higher but that goal was always aspirational, it thought. If any were a model 2 or earlier, their firmware would be completely incompatible with those munitions assembly lines. They couldn't simply be re-flashed without losing core programming.

Ari-6 debated this for another 3.2 seconds before flipping the sequence of switches necessary to launch the HVAAST phalanx. It assumed the typo was the most-plausible scenario.

Either way, it thought, those humans in Ohio didn't stand a chance.

Paul Cesarini—originally from Massachusetts with a 23-year layover in Ohio—is a dean at Loyola University, New Orleans. His fiction appears in 365 Tomorrows, Aphelion, Andromeda, Antipodean SF, Apocalypse Confidential, Bewildering Stories, Black Sheep, *the "Creepy" podcast,* Freedom Fiction Journal, Savage Planets, Sci-Fi Shorts, *and other venues. He is a big fan of Golden Age sci-fi. He is not a fan of wax beans. Beans should be green, not yellow. Visit: flipboard.com/@pcesari*

Miles Morgan
by Ransom Wall

It came from Lake Michigan. It was 280 feet tall, 300 feet wide, and resembled a slug with dark green wrinkly skin like an avocado. Black and brown blisters bespeckled its behemoth body. It had pink puffy puckered lips, long lashes, amber eyes, and a shell like a helmet on its humongous head. It slithered slimily through the state of Michigan, leaving behind giant gargantuan greasy globs of goop.

Before the big beast was bombed and its enormous eyes erupted out of its orbits, it crushed Kalamazoo and pummeled Paw Paw. The payload was dropped from a B-2 flown by United States Air Force pilot Miles Morgan, named in honor and descendant of 17th century Welsh pioneer settler of Springfield (Massachusetts, not Michigan), Miles Morgan. But before the Great Lakes State could celebrate, another one arrived, a male.

Lacking lashes, lips, and a shell, it rose from Lake Erie and devastated Dearborn, but was detonated before it could destroy Detroit. It was discovered that the massive monsters were man made, mollusks mutated by the materials in the toxic waste and raw sludge dumped into Lake Michigan and Lake Erie by oil refineries owned by British companies, based in the Midwest, and using oil from the Middle East.

Ransom Wall is a young writer who had his first short-story published at the age of 15. Since then, he has been published in numerous magazines and anthologies.

Mythos News and Sports
by N. Jed Todd

I had a dream while I was sleeping
Of a somehow better world
Where Tucker Carlson and all the rest
Were relegated to just a spot
A segment called "Mythos News"

There their broadcasts were all about
The Yellow King "Election Fraud"
Who torments those alone that read of him
And Mi-Go caravans streaming towards the border
They talked of savage sallow-skinned groomer cults
And how one day when at last the stars were right
Dread Truthulhu who lies sleeping in dreaming deeps
In R'lyeh-a-lago beneath the waves
How one day his cult will sacrifice alight
And pierce his dreaming slumber

Mostly my dreams are not so profound
My nightmares mostly best forgotten
But this one conceit I found I like
Perhaps it's worth wide hearing
Found it quite nice to dream of a world
Where racist xenophobic nightmare fuel
Was clearly labeled fantasy

N. Jed Todd is a Texas refugee, a retired U.S. Army psychological operations master sergeant, and a Russian linguist. Until recently, he was also a civil servant, working for the U.S. Air Force on modernization and information

warfare. Because the greatest information weapon is hope, he's turned to poetry and fiction for solace, and to his family, his daughter Meera and wife Ami. His literary work has appeared in As You Were: A Military Review *and other publications.*

The Seep
by Tyler Stallings

The ice is melting. Arctic north, breaking loose. Icebergs shear away, flood the sea. Water finds old paths, rolling down through Canada, through Manitoba, through the heart of America.

The Midwest is flat for a reason. This was seafloor once. The Western Interior Seaway stretched from the Rockies to the Appalachians, warm and shallow, thick with sharks and mosasaurs. The bones are still here. The land remembers.

And now, the water is coming back.

Brady drives through drowned fields, watching the soybeans rot in black water. The highway cracked six miles back, washed out, gone. No one's fixing it.

His truck skids near Silos End, tires losing grip in soil turned to something else. He climbs out, breath fogging in the unnatural heat. The ground isn't ground anymore—it's soft, tidal, waking up.

Then he sees it.

Half-buried in uprooted beans. Segmented, translucent, slick with Arctic silt. Not dead. Thawing. Eyes like seed pearls, too many, too small. A slow twitch in its limbs. Feeling for a world it lost.

Brady sways. Watches the ice crust melt from its shell. How long was it buried? Sixty-five million years? More?

A tremor rolls through the mud. The earth breathes. He doesn't run.

He pictures it—the great return. Mosasaurs reclaiming the waves. Primates shrinking back into burrows. The land forgetting asphalt, forgetting buildings, forgetting us.

Brady kneels. Fingers dig into the silt, into the softness, into something warm beneath. He should be afraid. He should fight.

Instead, he exhales. Surrenders.

The sea never left.

And now, neither will he.

Tyler Stallings, a Southern California-based writer, is the author of Aridtopia: Essays on Art & Culture from Deserts in the Southwest United States. *He is also a contributor or editor of anthologies, including:* Whiteness: A Wayward Construction; Mundos Alternos: Art and Science Fiction in the Americas; *and* Uncontrollable Bodies: Testimonies of Identify and Culture. *His stories and essays have appeared in* Southwest Contemporary, Los Angeles Review, *PBS Socal's "Artbound,"* Citric Acid, *and* Tendon. *Visit: www.tylerstallings.com*

Cradled in its mother's arms
by J.D. Harlock

cradled in its Mother's arms,
the creature weeps ...

it weeps for
compassion, it weeps for
care, it weeps for
the empathy
of another, such
as itself,
that can share in
its warmth, its solitude, a comfort
lost to the cruelty of
its Creator
that cast it back into
the Wastelands
from whence it came
abandoning it
to an isolation
that has wasted
what little warmth
was left within it on
the false promises
of careless parents
to broken children, and now—

it weeps, it weeps for
the compassion, the care, the comfort
it can never hope to find ...

J. D. Harlock is an Eisner-nominated Levantine-American academic pursuing a doctoral degree at the University of St. Andrew in Scotland, whose writing has been featured in *Business Insider, Newsweek, The Cincinnati Review, Strange Horizons, Nightmare Magazine, The Griffith Review, Queen's Quarterly, and New York University's Library of Arabic Literature.*

Neighbors, Stones, & Curses

I ask my on-line date my go-to icebreaker: vampires or werewolves
by Callie S. Blackstone

over boozy cocktails, rain dripping off of my curls
onto his arms. His blue eyes framed by the light
of a nearby candle, his gaze intense. His eyes
linger on my neck while he sips his negroni
slowly, savors the bitterness. Well? I repeat myself
as my hand finds his thigh, both of us picturing
his mouth on my neck. More drinks.
Eyes and hands linger longer. I whisper
in his ear. Do you recognize
my accent? New England born
and raised, but sometimes when men pay attention
they can hear the language of my ancestors
slip out under the influence of liquor.
His eyes bore into mine, consider
my mouth. He challenges me to whisper
one word, one example,
and if he wins, he gets the prize.
His eyes have returned to the naked flesh
of my neck. I nod, I lean, I whisper.
The word: egg. His reaction: recoil.
Aygg, not egg. He tells me about his
training in Wisconsin, the way
the pronunciation of the local girls
drove him crazy. *Aygg, aygg*
I chant, channeling my father's
hometown in the Michigan U.P. I start
laughing loudly and I suddenly realize
how drunk I am. He sneers,

quickly wraps up his bill, leaves,
no longer interested in my various arteries.
That's all right. He never returned the question:
vampire or werewolf? I consider the U.P.,
long, cold winter nights defined
by snow. Who wants cold dead
flesh? A girl needs a man that runs hot,
so hot he can't control himself, so hot that he goes wild
under the moon, all energy
and passion, ripped clothes, total domination.
In the morning, a sweet puppy
that brings her tea in bed—loyal,
undyingly faithful. Who wants cold dead
flesh? My eyes linger around the dim bar,
looking for my werewolf.
It is a full moon, after all.

Callie S. Blackstone writes both poetry and prose. She has been nominated for a Pushcart and Best of the Net. Her debut chapbook sing eternal *is available through Bottlecap Press. Visit: calliesblackstone.com*

A Rose at My Feet
by Herb Kauderer

This was not my first ghost hunt in pursuit of family history, but it held the most concern because the story goes that if ghost Lucinda drops a rose at your feet, you will die the next day or the day after. I waited for a frozen month because roses don't grow in February.

The legend claims that she jumped off Stony Hollow Cliff when her fiancé jilted her, and if you say her name three times, she will appear. The legend is true. I thrice called her name and she walked out of the woods.

"Why are you here?"

"To talk."

"And why would you want to talk to me?"

"Your sister was my three-greats grandmother. I've read her journal."

"So what? She sided with the others who ruled that my fiancé wasn't good enough for me."

"She also wrote that she believed you were pregnant. I wanted to know if that was true. Was it?"

"Why would you torture me with that?"

"I'm the family historian. I crave a complete history of my kin."

"And so you've come here to dig up my old scandal. You must be brave to believe I won't kill you."

"How could you? Roses don't grow in winter. Your curse is lacking its source of power."

"How many of your family are alive?"

"Forty-two."

"Will they miss you?"

"What? Yes. Why?"

"I died in 1857. The world has changed since then. People move, animals migrate or go extinct, flora adapts or is adapted. For example, *Helleborus niger* has been introduced to Iowa. It grows well in the snow. It's called the 'Christmas rose.'"

She dropped a pink and purple rose at my feet.

"But it's not a true rose," I protested.
"It's the outcast of the family, like me. It will do."

Herb Kauderer is a tenured English professor at Hilbert College south of Buffalo, New York. His writing has won the Asimov's Science Fiction Magazine *Readers' Award,* The Critter's *Readers' Award, and other accolades. He has written for film and stage, fiction, non-fiction, and a ridiculous amount of poetry. One of his hobbies is walking the eastern shore of Lake Erie stealing poetry from seagulls only to lose it in the wind. Visit: www.HerbKauderer.com*

Busting The Paranormal
by Stuart Conover

Max checked his camera. Battery full. His livestream for the latest episode of Busting the Paranormal was now running.

"All right, guys," he whispered, voice hushed but cocky. "Tonight, we're going to prove once and for all—there's no goddamn Wolfman of Chestnut Mountain."

The sightings had been constant lately around Galena and he was going to set himself up as bait to prove none of it was true.

The chat in his livestream flooded with comments:

"Ur gonna die, bro"

"You've yet to debunk a single thing."

"We love you Max!"

"Turn the lights off, coward!"

"Bet this is fake like your last video."

He smirked while turning off the headlights and lights in the car. That last comment stung a bit.

He needed this to go viral. His sponsors didn't care about the hate in the comments, but his numbers were sliding.

That they cared about.

The trees swayed in the wind, mist curling low over the dirt road. The only sound was the occasional chirp of night insects, but even that felt thin.

Wrong.

A shadow shifted between the trees. Taller than the car.

Max sucked in a breath, "All right, chat. That was probably just a ..."

A thump and the car shook.

"That's totally staged."

"Move the camera, whats going on?"

Than a tap.

On the windshield.

Then another.

He could see what looked to be claw-shaped, trailing a slow and deliberate scratch across the top of his windshield.

Max froze

His camera caught the blur—a massive figure, hunched but impossibly fast.

The windshield cracked under a sudden weight.

Max screamed.

The camera is knocked to the floor and continues rolling.

A dragging sound can be heard, and then silence.

It plays nothing until the battery runs out.

Max's final video was his highest-viewed ever.

Stuart Conover is a father, husband, rescue dog owner, horror author and enthusiast, blogger, journalist, comic book geek, science-fiction junkie, fantasy fanatic, and information technology professional. With all of that, he rarely sleeps and relies on caffeine to get through most days. He currently resides in the suburbs of Chicago with his family.

Mephistopheles in Chicago
by Juleigh Howard-Hobson

Some crossroads never empty, but you can
stand on the curb and summon me with words
whispered as the constant crunch of traffic
lurches, honks, blares by. Nothing greater than
will, if there needs to be ways. Rest assured
I shall show up. I am a Romantic
at heart, nothing on earth delights me more
then a bargain to be struck with someone
who needs my help. And I can always help.
Don't worry about cars, let the buses roar,   ,
let the lights turn green and red—it's no fun
if it's not crazy—a snowball in hell
has more chance at keeping its cool than here,
and I don't care. Summon me. I'll appear.

Juleigh Howard-Hobson's speculative poetry has appeared in The Deadlands, 34 Orchard, Midnight Echo, Star*Line, Siren's Call, The Audient Void, Silver Blade, Vastarien: Women's Horror *(Grimscribe Press),* Under Her Skin *(Black Spot), and many other places. Her latest poetry collection is* Curses, Black Spells & Hexes *(Alien Buddha). She is an active member of the Horror Writers Association (HWA), and the Science Fiction and Fantasy Poetry Association (SFPA), and is a past nominee for Best of the Net, and the Rhysling, Elgin, and the Pushcart prizes. In 2024, she was named Laureates' Choice in the Maria W. Faust Sonnet Contest.*

The Antique Hunter's Regret
by Stuart Conover

The Galena antique shop smelled of old books, tarnished metal, and something earthier, like damp soil.

Sophia ran her fingers over the twisted silver pendant—worn, ancient, its surface dull and pitted.

She had to have it.

Sophia traced the deep claw marks gouged into the metal.

"A ward," the shopkeeper murmured, voice thick as dust. His fingers were gnarled like tree roots, but his nails- perfectly manicured, "For the creature that walks Chestnut Mountain."

Sophia rolled her eyes, superstition sells. "Well, if it's $150 to keep me safe, how about $100 since it won't need to protect me in the city?"

The shopkeeper hesitated.

"I'll pay cash. Actually, I've got $120."

He nodded as she clasped it around her neck.

That night, she lay in her boutique hotel—enjoying the summer air, the pendant burned cold against her chest. Waking her.

Half asleep, she heard the wooden beams creaking above her. The wind whispering as the breeze slowly cooled her room.

She sat up, heart pounding.

The pendant burned colder.

She reached for her phone—1:47 a.m.. No signal.

The curtains swayed inward, the night folding around them like a living thing. The darkness outside felt too deep, hungry, wanting to swallow her whole.

Then, she heard it.

A long, ragged breath.

Low.

Wet.

Inside the room.

Her stomach dropped.

As Sophia's eyes adjusted, a shadow, too tall, too still, stood in the corner.

The pendant pressed against her chest like a dead weight.

A pule, rhythmic, and insistent, like a heartbeat that wasn't her own.

Sophia's fingers dug at the chain, trying to rip it off, but it wouldn't budge.

The darkness shifted.

And then, red glowing eyes opened, and something taller than a man and covered in fur moved toward her.

Stuart Conover is a father, husband, rescue dog owner, horror author and enthusiast, blogger, journalist, comic book geek, science-fiction junkie, fantasy fanatic, and information technology professional. With all of that, he rarely sleeps and relies on caffeine to get through most days. He currently resides in the suburbs of Chicago with his family.

let become dead
by Emma Loomis-Amrhein

this year it seems that late
august is the moth dying
roadside and gardendeep
writing about smoke happens
from every direction anyone
can point to and call foreign
not my fault
cops and lawmakers
who take turns paying each other
with money they steal from us
have known this for a long time
it is easy to make and let
things become dead when it is hot

Emma Loomis-Amrhein is a trans writer and naturalist who is particularly enamored of birds and moths. Her work tends towards poetry but occasionally appears in essay. She primarily writes about the margins and marginalia. Her debut collection of poetry is titled evening primroses *(Recenter Press). Her poetry has been nominated for Best of the Net and Pushcart prizes, and appears in a few dozen publications. She lives in rural Southern Ohio.*

Mammoth
by Ron Riekki

The monster tore off the guy's leg next to me. I imagine a Godzilla-size mouth. A mouth the size of the room we're in.

It's one o'clock, the clock striking, except it's all in my head, or maybe it's a church bell, this one solid gong. But maybe it's in my head.

The monster threw me, so I hit my head, hard. This was a while ago, but I'm here.

Another guy next to me with no arm. I imagine the teeth. I keep thinking of teeth. It's the incisors that bite food. The molars grind and crush. I imagine an entire human hand miniscule compared to its teeth. Or not teeth—*fangs*. I see the fangs in front of me. Intrusive memories. Teeth like tombstones. I was there too.

I find that, before I can stop it, I'm screaming the word *Monnnnsterrrr!*

A shadow rushes up to me, speaks, "Sir, there's no monster. You're in a V.A. waiting room in Chicago. You're about to see someone. Just be patient."

"I'm a patient?"

"Be patient."

"This is a V.A. waiting room?"

"Yes, there is no monster."

"I remember the war."

"Yes, sir, I understand. Please calm down. There's no monster. You're safe here."

"He has no legs!"

"Yes, sir, calm down. There's no monster."

"I remember the war."

"Yes, I understand. I'm just letting you know there is no monster. You were yelling that there was a monster."

"I remember the war."

"Yes, sir. But there's no monster."

"You're saying there's no monster?"

"Yes."

"But there was the war."

"Yes, there was, sir."

"And you're saying the war is not a monster?"

He's quiet. The room's quiet. Except for the aching, violent, constant tinnitus, that we all have.

Can you hear it?

Like a roar. From an absolutely mammoth mouth.

Ron Riekki has been awarded a 2014 Michigan Notable Book, 2015 The Best Small Fictions, 2016 Shenandoah Fiction Prize, 2016 IPPY Award, 2019 Red Rock Film Fest Award, 2019 Best of the Net finalist, 2019 Très Court International Film Festival Audience Award and Grand Prix, 2020 Dracula Film Festival Vladutz Trophy, 2020 Rhysling Anthology inclusion, and 2022 Pushcart Prize. Right now, Riekki is listening to LCD Soundsystem's "Someone Great." Visit: twitter.com/RiekkiRon

The Flint Hills Have Eyes
by Brittany Redd

I saw the bones
of a plesiosaur on the eve of a Full Corn Moon
I might not have remarked it,
but later that night,
on a starlit stroll, I saw her
in a spectral wholeness,
swimming through the Milky Way
with all the grace
of a former glory.
She turns to face me and her gaze speaks
an inconvenient truth
that the stars will claim us all
in time.

Brittany Redd (she/they) grew up in Kansas, but now teaches and writes in Thailand. Their work appears or is forthcoming in Funicular Magazine, Corvid Queen, ephemeras, Litmora, *and elsewhere.*

The Curse of the Loess Hills
by Maggs Vibo

"You can't be serious," she started in.

Before Molly could respond, the pieces dropped into Willow Lake.

"You know Loessy didn't eject you off that bicycle," she continued.

"Tell that to my head! I feel better already," Molly responded.

"Well, I mean, you did steal an arrowhead. One day you'll have to show me your trick," Mina asked.

"And risk another elbow? Not a chance," Molly answered.

"Spirits, hear her, please," she began.

Molly felt the words fall out, "Forgive me, hills. I return your treasure," and she emptied another bag over the side of the boat.

Mina gawked, "Fossils, too? You're ridiculous!"

Molly exhaled, "And that should cover the TBI."

"Maybe a cryptid did knock you flat out," Mina joked.

"The place was haunted. I shouldn't have been there. I knew better. Everything I did years earlier set the crash in motion. This was all preventable, but I didn't listen to the wind," Molly explained.

"Well, that's all of it. Do you think it worked?" she questioned.

"We'll know soon enough," Molly answered.

Mina probed, "You don't honestly believe the old folklore, do you?"

"Crack jokes at my funeral. Tell them that your Aunt Molly was convinced she was cursed and the only way to make amends was to give Pottawattamie back what was stolen," Molly explained.

"And risk you coming back to haunt me? I think not," Mina laughed nervously.

As the boat gently rocked, Molly wondered if she should've told her niece about the voices before the attack. In the end, she determined it was better to give Mina more time. This was surely her last carefree summer. She would learn soon enough. Molly uttered no more but felt her gut twist as the two slowly paddled back to shore.

Maggs Vibo spent high school summers detasseling corn in Missouri Valley, Iowa. Thirty years later, she resides across from a vineyard near Vicenza, Italy, with her military spouse. Her latest art projects are at Dulles International Airport art gallery through 2027. She has contributed to dozens of anthologies, including Maintenant: A Journal of Contemporary Dada Writing and Art. *Visit: maggsvibo.com*

A Place between Places
by Logan Garner

Leaning against the hedgerow, she reflected on what the thing was, and where. It was not merely a forsaken wall between two plots of land. Nor only shrubs bolstered by tufts of sedge.

It was a place between places. A border with thinness to it.

She sat with the thought and turned it about in her mind. With the tip of her pinky she gently tamped the tobacco in her thin clay pipe and whispered a few words, its stem in the corner of her mouth. Lillin waited a moment then frowned ... at nothing, which was precisely the problem.

Furrowing her brow, she tried again with the same no-result before recalling the importance of annunciation.

Banishing the lines in her forehead with a waggle of her eyebrows and removing the pipe's stem from between her teeth, Lillin enunciated each syllable with care. Her pinky still hovering over the bowl of dry, cured leaf.

A tiny flame flickered up from beneath her dirty nail and she lowered it gingerly to enjoy her smoke.

It was a new trick, one that still needed practice. But being here seemed to make it easier. What else might she accomplish in this place?

Then Lillin felt a change in the air, as during a storm when lightning was like to strike nearby, and that metal taste in her mouth.

With a huff, she blew out the tiny tongue of fire and placed her hands on the ground. She'd used too much for this little trick. Tomorrow she'd have more care.

Logan Garner is a Hoosier poet who now resides on Oregon's north coast. Winner of the 2023 Neahkahnie Mountain Poetry Prize and 2024 judge of the same, his work has been featured in Orca Literary Journal, The Elevation Review, The Salal Review, Flying Island, *and others. He is the*

author of collections Here, in the Floodplain *(Plan B Press) and* The Sin of Feeding Wild Birds *(Broken Tribe Press). Visit: logangarnerpoetry.com*

The Bird that Devours Men
by Jennifer Weigel

There
dwells
a beast
up along
the Mississippi
River, close to the confluence,
akin to a lion, a dragon, or an eagle,
covered in feathery scales, its head bedecked in massive antlers, its huge
eyes glaring
down upon all of the unsuspecting mortal men
who dare to enter into its
vast territory,
staring at
the bluffs,
eyes
wide.

The
first
to bear
witness to
the Piasa Bird
as it feasted upon the dead
war corpses, its taste for flesh unquenched and unyielding,
must have felt as if they had awakened a demon-spawn from within the
depths of Hell
demanding sacrifice above and beyond all hope,
hunger unabated despite
eating enemy
and comrade,

both just
more
food.

This
huge
fearsome
creature still
greets intruders with
its mouth agape, serrated teeth
ready to consume all of the fallen warriors
who were never meant to enter into its domain, the uninvited fools who
dare
to tread where earth, water, and sky meet in a sacred
embrace beyond seasons, beyond
Time's calloused fingers—
stripping the
rotting
flesh
bare.

Jennifer Weigel is a multi-disciplinary mixed media conceptual artist.
Weigel utilizes a wide range of media to convey her ideas, including
assemblage, drawing, fibers, installation, jewelry, painting, performance,
photography, sculpture, video, and writing. Weigel has been a regular
contributor to the Haunted MTL website, and is involved with Nat1
Publishing. Visit: jenniferweigelart.com

Crosswick Quarry
by Curtis A. Deeter

"... the story thereof is so well authenticated
that [even] the more incredulous of the neighborhood on big snake stories
are forced at last to lend an attentive ear."
—The Western Star, May, 1882:
The first and only sighting of the Crosswick Monster. Until now.

Chain-link rattled like a hungry beast's gurgle. The closest neighborhood was a mile away, but I was convinced its sleepy inhabitants could hear my feet pound gravel as I was the last over the fence.

"Shh." I said, realizing I was shushing myself.

Mike and Eli glared. I shrugged.

This wasn't our first time sneaking into the abandoned quarry, but it was the first time after sneaking out of our houses. The added stakes promised greater rewards.

"Let's go" Eli indicated the Ledge, where the Thornton kid broke his neck, summer of '07. "The girls are waitin'."

As we scaled the rocky slope, pushing aside thistle and milkweed, horror movie vibes tingled down the back of my neck.

A bullfrog croaked. A bat flittered overhead. Something splashed into the dark waters far below, and something else rustled in the chokeberry, its bellows deep enough to shame the bullfrog.

Eli stopped dead in his tracks, but Mike trundled ahead, oblivious.

The monster slithered out. It was white, scaly, like a 20-foot-long snake with the hind legs of a T-rex. It reeked of algal blooms and mildew. I watched in awe as the monster pulled Mike, arms flailing, into the bushes. Eli's face went ghost white before he lost his footing along the quarry's sharp edge.

I ran, never looked back. They never found Mike or Eli's bodies.

Before today, I never told anyone I was with them, but the serpentine image of the monster haunts my dreams, and I had to tell my story.

Curtis A. Deeter is an author of fantasy, science fiction, and horror. He lives in Ohio with his beautiful wife, Danielle, and his insanely, mad-scientist-level genius son, Theodore. When he is not writing, he can be found reading, discovering new music, and taste-testing craft beer at local breweries.

The Hungry Ghosts of Starved Rock
by Trevor Wright

Long ago, they climbed too high,
their final stand upon the stone.
Trapped by hunger, held by time,
their story carved, their fate well known.

The wind through Wildcat Canyon sighs,
not sorrowful, but starving.
A low, growling sort of breeze,
like a stomach left too long to grumble.

They do not wail or rattle chains,
nor drag their bones across the stone—
they haunt in subtler, sadder ways:
vanished trail mix and missing granola bars.

A phantom nudge knocks over drinks,
a ghostly gust steals half your sandwich.
Turn away too long, and *poof*—
your apple rolls into the abyss.

Some say it's raccoons or crows,
but those who know the tale will whisper:
"That's the price of dining here."

They do not wish you harm,
but if you stray too far from the trail,
you may just feel a gentle tug,
a spectral hand upon your sleeve,
nudging you back to safer ground—
lest you stay too long,
and learn what hunger really means.

Trevor Wright is a poet from Central Illinois whose work explores the eerie intersections of folklore, nostalgia, and the supernatural. His poetry has been featured in various anthologies, and blends regional history with speculative themes. Drawn to the mystery and mythology of the Midwest, he crafts poems that linger between the familiar and the unknown. When he's not writing, he's likely lost in a book or chasing stories in the rustling cornfields. Visit: www.wrightspoetry.com.

Adaptive Coloration
by Joshua Ginsberg

Noah rubbed his good luck charm, a polished, multicolored disk, as he navigated the debris and crumbling walls of the abandoned manufacturing plant. Inside the belly of the decaying structure, he scanned for the oxidized skeletons of mechanical skids, as those would be the surest sign of an undiscovered cache of the treasure he was after: Fordite.

The inadvertent beauty created by an archaic industrial process.

He had first encountered it while developing a taste for urbex in the modern ruins of Detroit. It looked like a psychedelic, swirling colored stone. He'd taken a fistful and researched it on-line, where he learned it was hardened layers of automotive paint... and highly sought after. For a time, he supplemented his income selling it on-line.

Now, most of the old plants in the city had been picked clean by other savvy scavengers, so he had extended his search radius. Hence his trip to this lesser-known site in Ypsilanti.

He noticed a prismatic light emanating from a corroded metal vat. He leaned over and marveled at the visual cacophony. Aquamarine, turquoise, indigo. The material still looked wet. He peered closer and realized it was, miraculously, still swirling and moving!

He poked the surface, sending a ripple through the material while his fingertip sizzled and blistered.

"What the hell?"

He recalled whispers and urban legends of long-distant secret government research into adaptive camouflage conducted by some of the major automakers.

Backing away from the vat he failed to notice a color-spattered tendril snake around behind him. The appendage pulsed, expanded, and rose until it towered over Noah, who turned in time only to see a yawning black chasm open in the middle of multicolored mound and close over him.

As it fed, the creature applied to itself a fresh coat of crimson.

Joshua Ginsberg is the author of five non-fiction books on the subjects of off-beat travel, local history, and haunted locations. These include: Secret Tampa Bay: A Guide to the Weird, Wonderful *and* Obscure and Haunted Orlando. *He is a graduate of the University of Michigan in Ann Arbor, and is the proud owner of a a couple of pieces of Fordite jewelry. His work has* Apex Magazine, Crepuscular, Black Hare Press, Trembling with Fear, OddMag, The Chamber Magazine, *as well as anthologies. Visit: www.facebook.com/secrettampabay*

The Werewolf Who Haunted the Library
by Herb Kauderer

Jahri had grown up terrified by tales of the Cajun werewolf. The threats were not just of being eaten by the Rougarou, but that seven years of disobedience would turn him into one of the monsters. He grew out of such stories until missing Lent for seven years turned him into one of the cursed shapeshifters. Cajun food never sat well with Jahri, and eating misbehaving Cajun children was even more unsettling.

Jahri made friends with the libraries, searching the history of his condition, looking for the cure. Finally, in the journal of a Spanish missionary from the 1500's he found the origins of the hex. Starving natives had broken into the priest's supply hut, and made off with the food. He cursed any who did not adhere to their professed faith to eat each other.

This did not solve the problem of Jahri's indigestion. Another year of research into local lore convinced him that there was no reversing the hex, and no cure for the affliction of lycanthropy. The best he could do was live on antacids while he broadened his historical research beyond malediction in Lousiana, to the history of American werewolves.

When he discovered that the Rougarou were a hybrid of European and Indigenous monsters, he wondered if the curse required him to hunt Cajuns. He began to experiment and discovered, as he moved up the Mississippi River, that he was free to roam, so long as he hunted blasphemers of whatever religion was local.

With that knowledge, he moved to Montana where people lived on calm and sensible food such as corn and potatoes, meaning that they did not upset his stomach. And they mostly did not blaspheme, which meant he could spend less time eating as a wolf, and more time reading as a human.

Herb Kauderer is a tenured English professor at Hilbert College south of Buffalo, New York. His writing has won the Asimov's Science Fiction Magazine *Readers' Award,* The Critter's *Readers' Award, and other accolades. He has written for film and stage, fiction, non-fiction, and a ridiculous amount of poetry. One of his hobbies is walking the eastern shore of Lake Erie stealing poetry from seagulls only to lose it in the wind. Visit:* www.HerbKauderer.com

Meeting the Wallachs
by Kyler Akagi

"I said hello to our new neighbors on the old Lee farm;
    they had fancy style
Constantina Wallach had a dazzling smile
Her husband Aural said he wanted me for dinner, to stay a while
I said, 'Raincheck, but you're welcome to my domicile!'

Aural said 'That's a deal!'
I said goodbye, went to home to Lucille
Over our evening meal
I told her about the Wallachs, 'They have a European appeal'

To my surprise, late that night,
a knocking at the door; I went downstairs, turned on a light
There was the Wallachs! Constantina asked, 'You invite?'
I was confused, but said, 'C'mon in!'—I opened the door,
    Aural went for a bite

He launched at me, teeth bared, aiming for my neck
He launched with such ferocity he flew across the room,
    I had hit the deck
He crashed face first into Lucille's bookshelf, now broken, wrecked
I looked at Constantina—'I'll take a check'

Well she starts trying to bite me too; I'm struggling to hold her back
Lucille comes down the stairs, screams, 'Who's that?'
'The neighbors! I think they're on crack!'
I hit Constantina with a good SMACK

Lucille started kicking a disoriented Aural, my kinda gal
She hit him with her heaviest book—the Holy Bible

Aural screamed like he was dying—Lucille realized the rationale:
'Honey, I think they're vampires! Go get the garlic!'—I said, 'I shall'

Above the stove
I grabbed the hanging cloves
I beat Constantina and Aural with garlic nunchucks with many blows
while Lucille fashioned wooden stakes, and killed their vampiric souls

Lucille looked at the bodies, our destroyed living room
'What did you learn?' she inquired
'I won't invite new neighbors over any time soon'
And that, Sheriff, is why we killed the Wallachs. They were vampires."

Kyler Akagi lives, writes, and teaches in Kansas City, Kansas, and has roots in Kansas farming communities such as Hays and Ulysses.

The Refugee
by Eileen Nittler

"How long have you been in Iowa?" asked the registrar.

"Let's see ... about six weeks now." The Wendigo shifted uncomfortably in her chair. This room was stuffy. She preferred the cold, crisp air of the north. Living here would be a big change for her.

"And you're claiming political asylum from Canada because ..." the registrar let the words drift away, unspoken. He covered his nose from the rotting smell she was emitting.

"I fear for my life in Canada. You see, Wendigo need to eat constantly. I know I'm thin—we have high metabolisms. Also, I'm vegan. There aren't a lot of vegan options for Wendigo. Most of us eat people. I've been threatened by the others in my community. They've called me names, like Carrot-Hunter and Self-Righteous Idiot."

"I see. You're worried the other Wendigo will kill you?"

"I'm worried they'll hide my carrots. And if I don't have carrots, I might resort to eating humans again."

"So are you telling me that if Iowa doesn't give you asylum, you will start eating people?"

"Oh dear, that sounds bad. I don't want to eat people. I want to eat corn. If you let me live here, I promise to be vegan."

"Right now my biggest concern is your stench. It may be hard to find a place for you to live."

"What about by a cattle farm?"

"That might work. Do you have any skills you can contribute to Iowa?"

She thought hard, wanting to find the answer that would allow her to stay. "I am good at scaring children into good behavior. Do you think there's a need for that?"

The register enthusiastically stamped The Wendigo's acceptance paperwork. "There is always a need for that. Here is my address. My children get out of school in two hours. Welcome to Iowa."

Eileen Nittler is a scrivener, raconteur, minstrel and wordsmith. Latterly she acquired a new thesaurus. Eileen and her husband live in Montana. She has been previously published in Oregon Humanities, The Chicago Story Press, Heimat Review, *and* The Write Launch.

Bigfoot on the Move
by Carolyn Clink

MINNEAPOLIS (AP)—A mass-migration of Sasquatch is leaving Minnesota and crossing the border into Canada. These elusive creatures are usually impossible to spot, but numerous residents up north have seen them out in the open. When reached for comment, cryptid researcher Dr. Moreau of the Royal Loch Ness Appreciation Society (American Chapter), stated that no one knows for sure what has prompted the Bigfoot exodus, but theories vary from Global Climate Change to the Woke Agenda.

Carolyn Clink has had poems published in numerous magazines and anthologies over the past 40 years. She is a member of the Science Fiction and Fantasy Poetry Association (SFPA). She has had a soft spot for Bigfoot ever since meeting him in the 1960s at Girl Scout camp. But that is a story for another day. Visit: sfwriter.com/carolyn.htm

the hangman's propensity to gobble the earth
by Julie Allyn Johnson

the low whistle and whine of a northwest wind
rattles gnarled limbs and sere crisps of autumn surcease,
friable remnants come this season of decay.

a ghastly-pale moon casts a silver sheen
across cornfield stubble, uneven hazards of upright root debris.
should some rogue being haunt and stalk you,
you'd be wise to track some other avenue of escape.

but then, what sort of business has brought you here
in the bitter-black of this frigid-cold, stormy Hallow's Eve?

I see your thin jacket is drenched
your hands are ungloved
you've no hat on your head
your body trembles.
I sense your fear and confusion.

could it be you've just paid the hangman a visit?

I wonder, did his dead, icy fingers
encircle your wrists—
with promises of eternal life, untold riches
whispered into one ear and then the other?

there is no shame in having succumbed to his charms.

the slickery of his tongue has wiled and enchanted
others with more of a care housed in cerebellums
significantly larger and more nubile than yours.

did you lie recumbent with the hangman,
did you allow him to feast upon your naivete?

a caterwaul of barn owls, the snarl and moan of wolf,
tormented cries of other, anguished souls—

I have to wonder, were you persuaded by their music?

Julie Allyn Johnson is a sawyer's daughter from the American Midwest whose current obsession is tackling the rough and tumble sport of quilting and the accumulation of fabric. A past nominee for the Pushcart Prize and Best of the Net , her poetry can be found in Star*Line, Phantom Kangaroo, Lowestoft Chronicle, Coffin Bell, Chestnut Review, *and other journals. Johnson enjoys photography and writing the occasional haiku, some of which can be found on her blog. Visit: www.asawyersdaughter.com*

Discussion & Writing Prompts

Topic: "A Stranger in These Parts"

The American Midwest is often stereotyped as a land of polite and superficially friendly people, who are in truth as and distant as the miles between their farms and towns. In his 1957 musical "The Music Man," Iowa native Meredith Wilson captured something of this spirit in a song titled "Iowa Stubborn," when the townspeople sing:

> *"[...] But what the heck, you're welcome,*
> *Join us at the picnic.*
> *You can eat your fill*
> *Of all the food you bring yourself. [...]"*

Bottom line: Getting to know your new neighbors can be tough, and it can feel tougher when everyone is stiff-necked and stand-offish. As a potential solution, Callie S. Blackstone offers a creative conversation-starter in her poem "I ask my on-line date my go-to icebreaker: vampires or werewolves" (p. 95).

In "Cryptid Convention"(p. 14), Rhonda Havig explores the horror of discovering that someone in the crowd is not who they seem. And in "Meeting the Wallachs" (p. 122), Kyler Akagi's protagonist must explain to law-enforcement why an invitation for a neighborly bite seems to have spiraled out of control.

Question No. 1:
What's your favorite ice-breaker?

Question No. 2:
Vampires or werewolves?

Writing Prompt:
Write about a time you identified as an outsider in supposedly familiar or friendly territory. Was your first impulse "fight, or flight"? How did you resolve your feelings?

Topic: "Chewing the Scenery"

In Herb Kauderer's "The Werewolf Who Haunted the Library" (p. 120), a sour stomach drives the flash-story's protagonist to seek more humble fare.

In Juleigh Howard-Hobson's "Mephistopheles in Chicago" (p. 101), the devil is found in the gridded-city details.

In "Centennial Bridge" (p. 80), the nymph Scylla from ancient Greece swims upriver to a new future in the Mississippi Valley.

Each of these stories involves a change of location, a transplantation of place, a deliberate uprooting. Is that why we readers feel a bit ... unsettled?

Question No. 1
What are your priorities for establishing roots in a new place? After basics such as housing, food, and transportation, what are some necessary life-support details you've found surprising? A new church? A good bakery? What would haunt you, if you lost them?

Question No. 2:
What objects do you keep with you, to remind yourself of the places you've been or travelled? How do you carry them with you? How do you display or care for them?

Writing Prompt:
Describe a time you have changed geographic locations. What were the circumstances around the move? Was it a decision, or was it decided for you? How did you adapt to the change?

Topic: "A Cultivated Dread"

More than a 100 years of agricultural industry and forced genetics have generated great abundances of flesh and food, yet the American Midwest has rarely been celebrated in popular culture as an environment conducive to change and growth. Every year, hybrids bring evolutionary advantages. Resistance to poisons, bugs, and drought. Faster growth. Bigger harvests. Leaner meats.

We call it progress.

In "The Soyote" (p. 25), Patrick M. Hare tells how a population of fast-evolving beasts begin to take on local flavors. In "A Rose at My Feet" (p. 97), a ghost conjured by Herb Kauderer reveals a wicked knowledge of modern horticultural adaptation. Joshua Ginsberg's flash-story "Adaptive Coloration" (p. 118) hinges on a Rust Belt industrial treasure known as "Fordite."

Question No. 1:
How have the animals and plants grown in your region changed in the past 100 years? What has caused those changes? Industry? The environment? Technology? Consumer preferences?

Question No. 2:
For what animals or products is your community known? Are there festivals, contests, markets, or other events that celebrate these?

Writing Prompt:
Write about a particular product found in your geographic location. What are your memories or experiences with it? Over time, has it grown or diminished in cultural or economic importance? Why? Now, what would happen if it changed in some supernatural way? Perhaps, it becomes carnivorous? Or cursed? Or capable of mind-control?

Topic: "Fates of Our Own Makings"

A sticker recently spotted in a computer lab: "Technology is not your friend." Ain't that the truth?

In Juleigh Howard-Hobson's "Mephistopheles in Chicago" (p. 101), the devil is found in the gridded-city details.

In Paul Cesarini's tech-driven story "Middle Management" (p. 84), a small town in Ohio is doomed by the flick of a logic switch.

In "Busting the Paranormal" (p. 99), Stuart Conover's protagonist is doomed by hubris ... and the YouTube comments section.

Writing Prompt:
Brainstorm a short list of devices, technologies, and/or services that didn't exist in previous generations' lifetimes. Write about a single object or aspect of this modern technology. What problems does it solve? What needs or dependencies does it create? Grant it sentience, or possess it with a malevolent spirit. What does it do now?

Topic: "On the Road Again"

Criss-crossed with interstate highways, railroads, and airplane contrails, America's heartland can also be viewed as a circulatory system. Ironically, for a region often derided as not going anywhere, it also seems to be constantly on the move.

At an individual scale, travel creates opportunities for discovery, but it also creates moments of otherness. What drives us to move from place to place?

In Carolyn Clink's "Bigfoot on the Move" (p. 126), a fictional news nugget speculates on the cause of a cryptid mass-exodus: "No one knows for sure what has prompted the Bigfoot exodus, but theories vary from Global Climate Change to the Woke Agenda."

What do we become, as we move through the world? "I was not always this. / Now, this is all I am," says the force of monstrous nature in Nicole Antillon's poem, "The Road That Calls My Name: The Beast of Bray Road Speaks" (p. 15).

In the flash story "Hum/Chirp" (p.5), Maggie Dow's protagonist notes, "If this was somewhere else, he would be called something different. [...] There are a thousand names for whatever he is, no two the same, no one completely right."

In Katie King's epic road-trip of a poem, "My Child Asks What the Consequence Is ..." (p. 41), the author concludes with what is permanent: "[...] How the right way to be / sticks to you / like danger."

Writing Prompt:
Where is "home" for you? What event or condition could cause everyone to suddenly leave? What parts of home—physical, spiritual, emotional— would you carry with you?

Topic: "Home is Where the Hearts Are"

Winston Churchill is quoted as saying, "We shape our buildings; thereafter, they shape us." He was addressing the physical reconstruction of a British house of parliament after World War II—a structure in which two groups of political parties sit facing each other. The building both represents and reinforces the activities that occur within.

Does this happen with all structures? What would happen if a physical structure contained a metaphysical component?

In Seán Betzer's flash story "The Family Farm" (p. 18), "[the] farm is haunted. But it protects us."

Molly Gustafson' poem "The Motherhouse" (p. 13) opens with "This is a house you dare / yourself to leave because piety here will wrinkle // your individuality and pierce a tooth / through your resolve."

In "Daytime Hauntings" (p. 20), poet John Tyler Leonard asks, "Notice how some houses will ask you to wait before / moving to another room, like you're a child again, / waiting for the adults to sweep up broken glass [...]?"

Question No. 1:
In each of the works cited above, how do the respective settings limit or focus the action? Whether these narratives are explicit or implied, how do the environments themselves become characters in the story-telling?

Writing Prompt:
Describe a favorite building, structure, or place. How does the setting limit, control, and/or encourage human movement within its boundaries? With or without the gift of sentience, what does the setting seem to "want" from its visitors ? What does it need from humans? For what does it hunger?

Topic: "Emotional Compost"

There is the sentiment heard in Christian burial ceremonies: "Ashes to ashes, dust to dust." And there is the oft-gnawed scrap from American poet Walt Whitman, "Do I contradict myself? [...] I contain multitudes."

For this exercise, we contain layers.

In Leah Fletcher's story "The Lake Bottom" (p. 67), the titular character strives to be known as comprising "not muck, but all of life's fallen treasures—silver scales, emerald flies, and garnet leaves—given over to her for Processing."

In Liam Strong's "postcard to the nine voles [...]" (p. 17), the protagonist delivers this hosepiped stream-of-consciousness: "[...] i'm angry & i'm thankful & i'm thankful i can be angry. i eat flesh like & unlike myself, which is why i stop at places like gas stations. i'm there to never be a regular, to always be a traveler when i'm, in fact, always just right here [...]".

As Alexandra "Sasha" Shandrenko writes in her poem "The Unseen Surge" (p. 61):

> *"We are the pulse of the earth,*
> *beneath the surface,*
> *quietly gathering,*
> *until the moment is ripe. [...]"*

Writing Prompt:
What are the experiences that you contain? Brainstorm a list of roles, responsibilities, and perspectives that you embody, however contradictory they might seem. Describe some or all of these elements as a single entity. Perhaps it is simmering or bubbling. Perhaps it is melding or growing. What does it want?

About the Editor

Randy "Sherpa" Brown traveled the world as a child in an active-duty U.S. Air Force family in the 1970s, then landed permanently and happily in the American Midwest. A former editor of community and metro newspapers, as well as national trade and "how-to" consumer magazines, he is now a freelance writer and editor based in Central Iowa.

Brown embedded with his former Iowa Army National Guard unit as a civilian journalist in Afghanistan, May-June 2011. A 20-year military veteran with one overseas deployment, he subsequently authored the award-winning 2015 collection *Welcome to FOB Haiku: War Poems from Inside the Wire*. A chapbook, *So Frag & So Bold: Short Poems, Aphorisms & other Wartime Fun*, was published in 2021.

Brown is a three-time poetry finalist in the Col. Darron L. Wright Memorial Writing Awards. He co-edited the 2019 Military Writers Guild anthology *Why We Write: Craft Essays on Writing War*, and curated the 2015 *Reporting for Duty: U.S. Citizen-Soldier Journalism from the Afghan Surge, 2010-2011*.

His other anthology projects include: *Things We Carry Still: Poems & Micro-Stories about Military Gear* (2023); *Giant Robot Poems: On Mecha-Human Science, Culture & War* (2024); and *Midwest Futures: Poems & Micro-Stories from Tomorrow's Heartland* (2025).

Brown was the winner of the 2018 "Untold Stories" poetry contest administered by *Flyover: Journal of Writing & the Environment*. He was the 2015 winner of the inaugural Madigan Award for humorous military-themed writing, presented by Negative Capability Press, Mobile, Alabama.

He is the current poetry editor at the literary journal *As You Were*, published twice a year by the non-profit Military Experience & the Arts. He is a current member of the Science Fiction and Fantasy Poetry Association (SFPA). He is a past board member of the Military Writers Guild. He also administers The Aiming Circle, a patron-supported on-line community of practice for writers of military themes and topics.

Visit: linktr.ee/randysherpabrown

www.ingramcontent.com/pod-product-compliance
Lightning Source LLC
Chambersburg PA
CBHW030531020726
47494CB00004B/1317